MAR

The Daughters of Allamont Hall

Book 4.5

A Regency Romance Novella

by Mary Kingswood

Published by Sutors Publishing

ISBN: 978-1-912167-23-4 (paperback)

Cover design by: Shayne Rutherford of Darkmoon Graphics

Mary: The Daughters of Allamont Hall Book 4.5

About this book: *A traditional Regency romance, drawing room rather than bedroom.*

Mary Allamont was resigned to spinsterhood, quite happy to keep house for her father and unruly brothers, until her step-mother returned to disrupt their lives. Then an eligible match failed when it was engulfed by an old family scandal. Now she's desperate for any way to escape, but an unexpected proposal might bring her more challenges than she can cope with.

Daniel Merton gave up the possibility of a career or marriage to support his friend, Sir Osborne Hardy, whose life is dominated by his mother and sisters. Now Osborne wants to help a lady in distress, and Daniel is just the man to smooth the way. But if he helps his friend to happiness, must he give up his own chance of love?

About The Daughters of Allamont Hall: a series of six traditional Regency romances, featuring the unmarried daughters of Mr William and Lady Sara Allamont. When their father dies unexpectedly, his will includes generous dowries for the sisters, but only on condition that they marry in the proper order, the eldest first.

Book 1: Amy
Book 2: Belle
Book 3: Connie
Book 4: Dulcie
Book 4.5: Mary (novella)
Book 5: Grace
Book 6: Hope

Table of Contents

1: Mothers

It took every ounce of Mary's willpower to stand motionless, head bowed, under the onslaught from her step-mother.

"What a fool you are, Mary! Seven and twenty, and no husband to be seen, and not even a suitor or two circling around. What am I to do with you? And if you will not even *try* for a little style, there is no hope for you, and you must resign yourself to spending the rest of your life a spinster. *Mon dieu*, what a wilful child you are! When I was barely sixteen, I had already received three offers, and..."

Mary shut her mind to it as best she could. She had heard the tales of her step-mother's days of glory many times, and the general abuse she could tolerate quite well now. It had begun so beguilingly well, too. They were sitting in the tiny drawing room of the Dower House, Mary sewing, and her step-mother leafing through the latest journals from London, when she had come across a new way of dressing hair.

"Come here, Mary. Look at this. It would suit you, *non*? These curls would take work, but it could be done and think how well you would look with such a modish style."

Obediently, Mary had looked, but could not help exclaiming in horror at such an outlandish arrangement.

"But it is all the crack in town, I am sure."

"It may be *'all the crack'*, as you call it, but it would make me look like a windswept goose girl, I am sure," Mary said. "I am very content with my present ways of arranging my hair."

And that had been enough to set off a tirade of venom from her step-mother. Mary had stood in silence, allowing it all to flow over her. But sooner or later, she knew, they would come to the greatest cause of her humiliation.

"And as for your most recent escapade — I shall not dignify it with the term *'betrothal'*, for it was no such thing — your position as the most laughed-at girl in the county is assured. Ha! That is so like you! All these years you will not marry this one or that one, but when you do choose, you make such a mess of it that he leaves again almost instantly! Such a good joke! I cannot remember when I have been so well entertained. *Betrothed*! You will never find a husband, never."

She laughed raucously, a harsh, grating sound. Mary winced, and even though she had heard the same complaint many times over, it still cut her deeply. It was so unjust, for she would never have considered Lord Kilbraith's offer if she had not been desperate to escape a home made unbearable by her step-mother.

"Betrothed — and then not!" She shrieked with laughter, until Mary could bear it no longer.

Her head lifted. "At least it would have got me away from *you*."

Her step-mother only laughed all the harder, but her eyes gleamed in triumph. Finally, she had provoked Mary into a response.

Mary spun in a swirl of skirts and strode to the door.

"Do not run away from me," her step-mother called after her, but Mary swept out of the room and slammed the door behind her. In the hall, she paused, breathing deeply for a moment. If only the house were larger! When they had had the whole of Willowbye to live in, she could always find a quiet corner to herself, where she could sit and reflect and compose her thoughts for the next task. But then, she had seldom needed to compose her thoughts, in those days. She had been mistress of the house, and very happy to be so. Marriage had never entered her thoughts.

But then the money had run out, Willowbye had had to be let, and now they all lived in the Dower House, which was wholly inadequate. And her step-mother, who had abandoned her family for many years, had returned to torment them all. But no — that was not entirely true. Her father seemed contented enough, and her brothers did as they pleased. It was only Mary who was the focus of her step-mother's poisonous dislike.

Her footsteps led her, as they so often did these days, to the Willowbye stables. Here resided the last trace of her betrothed, who had been discovered to be her brother, that little secret of her father's from so many years ago. As a token of their brief engagement, Lord Kilbraith had gifted Mary his splendid horse, Majestad, and he was her delight and her comfort. She could bury her face in his soft mane, and whisper all her grievances into his ear, and he would listen patiently and rest his head on her shoulder. He was a wonderful creature, a Spanish breed and pure grey, and the best of it was that he was so spirited that her step-mother did not dare to ride him. He was Mary's alone, the only thing in the whole world that was completely and unreservedly hers.

She had not been in the stables more than a few minutes when she heard hooves crunching across the gravel drive, and her father arrived on his hunter, a fine, mettlesome animal almost the equal of her own.

"Mary? Are you quite well?" he said, as he slid out of the saddle. "Do not tell me that you have quarrelled with Vivienne again."

She sighed, and Majestad huffed as if in sympathy. "I never mean to, you know that, but sometimes — she riles me, I confess."

"I wish you two could get on a little better," he said, although his tone was not unsympathetic. "She is not easy company, but if *I* can manage to rub along with her, I should think you could too, if you tried a little harder."

Tears welled in Mary's eyes, and she leaned her face against Majestad to hide her weakness. "I do try," she said, her voice muffled. "I try so hard, but she is so... so provoking, sometimes."

"She is a little prickly, it is true," he said, but without conviction.

Mary said no more. Her step-mother was devious, presenting a placid facade to her husband, and addressing her sons with amused tolerance. To Mary, however, the daughter who was not hers, she showed no mercy, although only when no one else was present. Her barbs were far more subtle in company.

"I shall go out for a ride," she declared.

"It is likely to rain," her father said. "Are you sure?"

But she was already on her way to change into her riding habit.

~~~~~

Sir Osborne Hardy was a baronet, master of Brinford Manor and its extensive demesnes, and possessor of a large fortune. Nor was he deficient in wit or learning. But his courage might be called into question by anyone who saw him quaking like a schoolboy before his own mother. Lady Hardy was a head shorter than her son, and so slender of frame that he could easily make two of her. Yet he shivered and wrung his hands and cast desperate glances at the door and the prospect of escape.

"It is high time, Osborne," Lady Hardy said in severe tones. "You are one and thirty now, and you cannot postpone the matter any longer. I have written to Lord and Lady Spilsby to propose that they bring Miss Grantham for a visit. Naturally there will be other guests but—"

"A house party?" Sir Osborne said, a rising tone of panic in his voice. "Not at m'best at parties, Mama, you know that."

"Really, Osborne," his mama said sharply. "Are you a gentleman or not? All that is required is for you to be your usual affable self. I shall do everything else that is needful, you may be sure. There will be a great deal of work for me, undoubtedly, but for my only son and the succession of the family name, no exertion is too great."

A small cough emanated from the sofa behind Lady Hardy, and the weathered face of Osborne's youngest sister Clarissa peered over her spectacles at him. "We shall help, too," she said in her gruff voice. "We have managed to hold a few house parties in our time."

"Oh, yes indeed we have. A great many, in fact," said his oldest sister, Ruth, her voice a mere thread.

It was an unhappy circumstance of Osborne's life that his sisters were not of his own age, as might be expected. Thirty years separated him from Clarissa, making her the same age as his mother. As Clarissa and Ruth had never married and had therefore always lived at Brinford Manor, and as both
~~~~~

had doted on little Osborne as he grew, he felt somehow as if he had three mothers. It was difficult enough to oppose his true mother, when she had her mind set on an object, and when all three of them lined up against him, the matter became well-nigh impossible.

And if by some miracle the power of the three failed, they would summon the relief troops of his two married sisters, Violet and Winifred. These two, trailing their burgeoning families, could be depended upon to visit frequently, descending whenever there was some crisis, real or imagined, which required the full might of womanhood to keep Sir Osborne on the right path. No dragon-slaying hero of the sagas or knight in arms from history could withstand the onslaught.

Today, however, Lady Hardy was in full flow, and no support was required.

"I hope I can manage a house party unassisted," Lady Hardy said loftily, glaring at her step-daughters. "As mistress of this house, that is my duty and as everyone knows, I never shirk my duty. There, that is all settled."

Daniel Merton stood, unregarded, in his corner of the room, watching in silence. The ladies rarely spoke to him, beyond the merest commonplaces. His official role was as Osborne's secretary and estate manager, but in practice he was a companion, supporter and bulwark against the perpetual onslaught of feminine pressure. And friend — he was Osborne's only real friend.

The room they were in was known as the smoking room, so designated by Sir Osborne's grandfather, also named Osborne. The room was still so described, although no one had smoked in there since the old man had died, many years ago. It was situated in a far corner of the house, and intended to be Sir Osborne's refuge, but his mother thought nothing of barging in whenever she had something important to say to him, which was often.

Osborne looked helplessly at Daniel. "What do you think, Danny?" he pleaded.

But Daniel knew better than to speak against Lady Hardy. "It will do no harm to meet Miss Grantham. You never know, she might be just the young lady to steal your heart."

Osborne looked doubtful.

"The decision remains yours," Daniel said, more firmly. "If you take her in dislike, you need not marry her. There are plenty of other young ladies equally suitable."

Lady Hardy glowered at him, but Osborne nodded eagerly. "Indeed, indeed. Plenty more. No need to marry this one, if I don't choose. Plenty more."

With a harrumph of displeasure, Lady Hardy withdrew in a rustle of violet bombazine, for she still liked to wear mourning colours in honour of her husband, although he had been dead for six years.

"Well, brushed through that tolerably well," Osborne said, hurling himself into a wing chair. "Lord, but m'mother's determined to see me leg-shackled, and there's no denying her. Never could say no to her."

"No man can ever say no to his own mother," Daniel said with a smile. "Besides, she has your interests at heart. Brandy?"

"Excellent idea! You are the best of good fellows, Danny, the very best. But what's a man to do? You know what m'mother's like — no rest until she gets her way. Have to do it, I suppose."

"You do have a responsibility to marry and continue the family line," Daniel said, handing Osborne a glass of swirling amber. "For a man in your position, it is a matter of duty. Still, you can choose the lady to please yourself."

"But how can I choose? I'm a sorry case, Danny — not much of a one for the ladies. I like a dance well enough, but when it comes to talking to them…"

"Then choose one who also dislikes talking. Or one who chatters away, and will relieve you of the need to say anything." Osborne winced. "Well, perhaps not that. But you may have the choicest of society's most eligible debutantes at your feet — indeed, you *do*, every time you go to London."

"Lord, yes, but they terrify me," Osborne said earnestly. "So fashionable and stiff, and they look me up and down as if I might be a prime piece of horseflesh they're contemplating buying. Sets me on edge, I don't mind admitting."

Daniel laughed and shook his head. "Ozzy, there is no doing anything with you. If you will not choose for yourself, then marry Miss Grantham and be done with it. At least your mama will stop hounding you."

"So she would! Have to, really. Do you think I should marry Miss Grantham, then? Advise me, Danny. You're so clever, tell me what I should do."

"If I were to advise you, I would say *not* Miss Grantham, because any wife chosen for you by your mother is likely to be a meek, timid little thing, quite unable to stand up to her. Remember when she hoped Miss Amy Allamont would do for you? That almost happened, too, except that Ambleside snatched her away at the last minute. With a wife like that, your mama would continue to rule the roast here. What you really need, I feel, is a wife who would manage everything here for your comfort, so that nothing would trouble you, not even your mother. The Manor would revolve around you, with your every wish attended to, as it should be. Nothing would be done that was not of your choosing, or to promote your happiness. That is the sort of wife you need, to my mind."

Osborne's eyes widened at this glorious prospect. "Oh, yes," he breathed. "But where is such a paragon to be found?"

"Not amongst the *haut ton* in London, that much is certain, and perhaps not amongst the ladies around here, who are already known to your mama. But perhaps in Bath?"

"Bath! The very place! I like Bath very much — such clean streets. We could take one of those pleasant houses near the Pump Room. Could take the waters again, for m'health, you know. Been feeling a little under the weather lately. Bath! Should find someone to suit me there, I daresay. But how shall I know? If a lady can... you know, stand up to Mama?"

"So long as *you* choose her, Ozzy, and not Lady Hardy, then your approbation will automatically give her the authority she needs, as your wife."

"Approbation. Certainly. Authority." But his eyes had acquired the look of panic again.

"Choose someone who is comfortable to be with, like a friend. She will be a confident mistress of the Manor by the mere fact that you have chosen her above all other women."

"Ah! Comfortable. Like a friend. Excellent! What would I ever do without you, Danny? A little more brandy, if you please. And if it is not raining, will you order the carriage. I feel like a little fresh air."

2: An Encounter

Sir Osborne's idea of an outing in the fresh air involved sitting in a closed carriage, well-supplied with rugs and hot bricks, and with the blinds raised and lowered at every turn to prevent the least penetration by dazzling sunshine. Eventually, however, he was comfortable enough to relax and the swaying lulled him off to sleep.

Daniel watched the scenery roll by, the bare fields and leafless trees uninteresting at this time of year. At each junction he communicated with the coachman the direction to take by means of a series of gentle taps on the roof, to avoid waking Osborne, keeping to the quiet lanes and avoiding the busy toll roads, with their fast-moving long-distance coaches and loud horns. The coachman knew to drive at a slow pace for the comfort of the occupants, but even so they had travelled some miles when it began to rain. It was fortunate that Osborne was asleep, or otherwise the weather would have thrown him into turmoil, for fear of becoming mired or even — the most unspeakable horror of all! — overturned.

They were nearing a point at which it might be possible to turn back when Daniel caught sight of something through the rain — a horse, a rather striking grey, and standing alongside it a dark-clad shape which could only be a lady in a riding habit. There was nothing untoward about a lady out riding, even unaccompanied and in such inclement weather, but there was something about the situation that struck him as odd.

He banged on the roof of the carriage, which lurched to a halt.

"Mmnph?" muttered Osborne, opening his eyes. "Danny? Are we home?"

"Not quite. There is a lady here, and I am not sure—"

"I see her. But look at this rain! She should not be out riding in such weather. Great heavens, she might take a chill, and at this time of year—! Why is she not riding her horse, Danny? And who is she, out all alone?"

"I believe it is Miss Mary Allamont, Osborne. No one else has a horse quite like that fine animal."

"Pray see if she needs our aid. Most concerned, you know, most concerned. Must be soaked to the bone in this weather. Do go at once — I shall cover m'self with the rug while you open the door, so no need to be anxious on my account."

Daniel stepped down into the mud, and splashed across to the tree which was providing a little shelter for horse and rider. She watched him approach, wiping her wet face with one sleeve. He could not be sure, since water dripped from her hat and wet hair, but he thought she might have been crying.

"Miss Allamont? Are you in trouble? Sir Osborne has sent me to enquire if you need any assistance."

"Oh, Mr Merton, how good of you to leave your carriage in such weather. Please thank Sir Osborne for his solicitude, but I shall manage very well. My horse has cast a shoe, nothing worse, I assure you. I have only to walk him home across the fields."

"We must be three miles from Willowbye, and in this rain—"

"Oh, not much above two, I am sure. Please do drive on, Mr Merton. Do not delay on my account, I beg you." Even as she spoke, a tear rolled unmistakably down one cheek and there was a catch in her voice which told of her distress.

"Miss Allamont, there is no power on earth which would persuade me to leave you to walk home alone. Let me acquaint Sir Osborne with your situation, and then we can send him on his way and I will accompany you home."

"No, please, you must not—"

But he turned away and strode back to the carriage.

Osborne was horrified. "Nonsense! Permit a lady to walk three miles in such dirty conditions? On no account! The groom may walk the horse home, and we will take Miss Allamont up in the carriage. I do not regard a little water, you know. I shall wrap myself up in the rug and there will not be the least speck of mud afflicting me."

With only a few minutes required to explain the shortest route to the groom, Miss Allamont was handed into the carriage, and Daniel squeezed in beside her, both of them keeping as far from Osborne as was humanly possible.

"You are so kind, Sir Osborne," she said. "This is beyond anything. I cannot express—" And then the tears were flowing and she could say no more.

Daniel hastened to find a handkerchief, but Osborne was there before him. "My dear Miss Allamont, you must not distress yourself so. We shall have you home safely in no time at all. How long will it take, Danny?"

"If the Brafton ford is passable, no more than half an hour."

"Ford?" Osborne said, paling. "Would it not be safer to pass through Brinchester?"

"That would take more than an hour," Daniel said.

"Then..." He swallowed hard. "Then we must risk the ford, for Miss Allamont's sake. Sitting about in wet clothes is most injurious to health. You must have a hot bath immediately you arrive home, Miss Allamont, and some broth or a posset. Brandy or Madeira is excellent, too, as a preventative. Danny, pull that rug a little closer about her shoulders. Are you cold, Miss Allamont?"

"Not at all, Sir Osborne, I thank you. I beg your pardon for my weakness. I have had... a trying day, and Majestad losing a shoe was the final straw." But still the tears flowed.

Osborne looked helplessly at Daniel.

"Miss Allamont," Daniel began tentatively. "Has anything out of the ordinary occurred to distress you? For I do not think you weep for the loss of a horseshoe."

"Nothing out of the ordinary, unfortunately," she said in a low voice, sniffing a little. "My life is not as comfortable as it might be, just now, but nothing can be done about it. I cannot escape, so I must bear it as best I can."

"We are aware of your difficult situation," Daniel said. His heart went out to her. He had known the family for many years, and it tore him apart to watch a sensible, intelligent lady reduced to such despair.

"Indeed," Osborne said. "All our sympathies, Miss Allamont. All our sympathies. Most trying for you."

The carriage began to rattle over uneven stones, rendering all conversation at an end. Daniel was seated beside Miss Allamont, watching her covertly as she sat and gradually composed herself, her back ruler-straight. What an admirable woman she was, so brave under duress.

Before long, they arrived at Willowbye and set Miss Allamont down at the Dower House. Daniel escorted her to the door, waiting only to ensure that she was safely received before returning to the carriage.

"Must we pass through the ford again?" Osborne said.

"I have instructed Harold to take us back through Brinchester," Daniel said, with a smile. "It is not a great deal further, and the road is so much better. You will be more comfortable. Are you warm enough, Ozzy?"

"Only slightly chilled. So much dampness! Careful where you sit, Danny! Need to dry the squabs thoroughly before we take this carriage out again. Cannot be too careful."

"Harold knows what to do. At least we returned Miss Allamont home safely. It was a gallant gesture, Ozzy."

"Gallant — really? Well. Must look after a lady, eh?"

Osborne was silent for so long that Daniel began to wonder if he had nodded off again, but when they came onto the toll-road and stopped momentarily, he said with unusual seriousness, "Not right, you know. That step-mother of hers makes her life a misery. Always liked Miss Mary Allamont. Used to be a pleasant, friendly woman. Now — *cowed*, Danny. Don't like to see a lady cowed like that. And today — crying like that. Lady should never be reduced to tears. Not right."

Another long silence.

Then he burst out, "Cowed m'self. M'mother cows *me* so I know how it is. Poor lady! She needs rescuing and no mistake. Pity that fellow Kilbraith never worked out. What went wrong again?"

"Some confusion over the dowry," Daniel said cautiously, for he had never believed the story put about to account for the abrupt ending of the betrothal. "Lord Kilbraith misunderstood, thinking that all the Miss Allamonts had large dowries, whereas in fact it was only Miss Mary Allamont's cousins who were so provided."

"Ah. Although — pretty well set up, by all accounts, Kilbraith. No reason for it to matter."

"Indeed," Daniel said, non-committally.

Silence again, as the carriage slowed to negotiate the traffic on the crowded streets of Brinchester. The rain had almost stopped, and the townsfolk had emerged from their houses to scuttle about completing their business before dusk fell.

As the town disappeared behind them and they came to open countryside, Osborne said timidly, "Had an exciting idea, Danny."

Daniel's heart sank a little. Osborne's exciting ideas usually turned out to be wildly impractical. He had once wanted to have a canal built around the perimeter of the Manor, so that he might enjoy the delights of boating while never being more than a yard from the shore. Another time, it had been a glass roof over most of the pleasure gardens which had captured his imagination, for then he might take his exercise and never be rained upon. It had taken all Daniel's powers of persuasion to talk him out of that particular scheme.

But he forced a smile. "Tell me all about it, do."

"Been thinking. I need a wife. Miss Mary Allamont needs a husband." Long pause. "What do you think?"

Daniel tried not to look surprised. As one of Osborne's exciting ideas, it was manifestly less outrageous than most. Indeed, it had some merit. Mary Allamont was a good sort of girl, old enough to be sensible and young enough to be still handsome, neither dowdy nor formidably fashionable. She had been mistress of Willowbye for a number of years before her step-mother's return, so managing Brinford Manor would not be beyond her. Nor would Osborne's mother dismay her. She had no authority over her own step-mother, but as Lady Hardy she would know how to deal with her mother-in-law.

"Ah." Osborne sounded disappointed. "Don't like the notion, then? Thought you rather liked the lady."

"Certainly I do. She is admirably suited to the role, but what made you think of her? You have known her for ever, after all, and never once has the idea of matrimony come into play. This is more than just sympathy, I trust."

"You told me to choose someone *comfortable*, like a friend, and that's just how she is — like a friend. Most young ladies — terrifying. Never know what to say to them. But *she* is easy to talk to. Feel *safe* with her, you see. Admirably suited, eh? And you *do* like her, I know y'do. Always talking about her."

Daniel took a breath. Then another. Yes, he liked her. She was exactly the sort of woman he would have wanted for himself, if he could have afforded to marry — if he had been the eldest son and not the youngest of five, or if his rich uncle had chosen him as heir instead of his middle brother, or if he had taken that commission in the army and made a fortune from the war. But instead he had chosen an easy life with Osborne, which had many compensations, but also some restrictions. Not for him the comfort of a wife, or the joy of his own children at his feet. For a moment, he was consumed with envy of his friend, free to turn his gaze wherever it pleased him, and when it came to rest, to say — there, that is the woman I shall marry. And it would happen, for she could hardly refuse.

"Everyone likes Mary Allamont," he said quietly.

"Then you approve? A capital notion, no? But what must be done? Should discuss it with m'mother first."

"No!" Daniel said hastily. "Not a good idea, Ozzy. If she disapproves — and she will — you will be back to Miss Grantham. If you are set on this, then offer for her."

"Offer for her." The panicked look was back in Osborne's eyes. "Just... go and... and *offer* for her? But what would I say?"

"I can suggest some phrases, if you wish, perhaps prepare a little speech for you to learn. Should you like me to do that?"

"What about you going instead?" Osborne said. "Always so good with words, you know the best things to say."

"Well... I can hardly go and offer on your behalf," Daniel said. "That would never do. But there might be a way. It would be perfectly acceptable for you to write to Miss Allamont to make your declaration and proposals, and I could certainly convey your letter to the lady."

"A letter!" Osborne said, his relief palpable. "Oh, an excellent idea. A letter — and you can help me compose it, Danny."

"Of course. I shall be happy to suggest the most felicitous wording."

"Excellent! Are we nearly home? Getting quite chilled now. Hope Worthing has plenty of hot water ready for m'bath."

3: A Proposal

For once, Mary had the Dower House to herself. Her father was at Willowbye, discussing the ongoing repairs with the builder. Her oldest brother, James, was out riding, Mark was away on his preaching rounds with his friend, and the youngest, Hugo, was for once usefully employed helping with the accounts at their cousins' house, Allamont Hall. Best of all, her step-mother had taken the carriage to Brinchester to look at muslins and cottons for the summer, and would be gone all day.

Mary had spent an hour in the pantry with the cook, counting jars and bottles, checking cheeses and spices, and deciding how best to eke out the supply of tea until the end of the month. Then she had examined the contents of the linen cupboard with the housekeeper. Now she settled down in her father's study to go through the accounts, for he was not very careful with his numbers and often made a mistake.

When she heard the knocker sounding at the front door, she sighed. It was not a day when callers might be expected, but sometimes they came anyway. How she longed to live in town where one might be 'not at home', and irregular visitors would be obliged to leave a card and go away. But Willowbye was so remote, and the journey through narrow, boggy lanes so uncomfortable that no caller could be turned away.

The butler knocked and entered. "Mr Daniel Merton to see you, madam. Shall I light the fire in the drawing room?"

"Mr Merton? Alone? Sir Osborne is not with him?"

"Alone, madam."

"In that case, you may show him in here. I daresay he has brought us an invitation from Lady Hardy, and will only stay a few moments. No point lighting another fire for such a brief stay." It also saved her from the displeasure of her step-mother over the indulgence of an extra fire.

She stood, smoothing her skirts, but she had not long to wait. The distance from the entrance hall to the study was no more than thirty paces.

"Mr Merton, madam," the butler intoned.

She curtsied, and he bowed. He was dressed, as always, in sombre clothes, well-cut without being flamboyant in style, of good quality without ostentatious extravagance. He looked the epitome of a quiet country gentleman, or a parson, perhaps. His features were regular, and that was all that might be said of them, but there was an intelligence in his dark eyes which gave him an air of great understanding.

After the usual exchange of greetings, he said, "I am glad to find you alone, Miss Allamont."

That startled her, and she coloured a little. A man — a *single* man — would only wish to be alone with a woman for one very particular reason, namely, that he were about to offer for her. Yet she had never heard that Mr Merton had the income to support a wife. He was quite dependent on Sir Osborne, she had thought. But then a man's circumstances might change overnight, with an unexpected death in the family. Whatever had happened, he would have his say, and she must wait patiently for him to get through it.

"I have brought you a letter from Sir Osborne."

That was so unexpected that her head was swimming. Surely Sir Osborne would not—? But no, it must just be an invitation of some sort, surely. Sir Osborne had never even looked at her. She remembered their meeting the other day in the rain — of course, he was merely making solicitous enquiries after her health. How gallant he was!

"That is very kind of him to write," she said. "However, there was no need."

"No need?" Now it was Mr Merton's turn to look surprised.

"None in the world, for such sentiments may be conveyed just as well verbally, do you not agree? And you may take my answer back to Sir Osborne, with my thanks."

"I... But of course, Miss Allamont, if you wish it. You have your answer prepared already?"

"Indeed. You may tell Sir Osborne that I am most grateful for his attentions, but I am quite well, and have taken no harm from my misadventure in the rain."

He smiled, and then, as if his merriment could not quite be contained, gave a little rumble of laughter. "I believe we may be at cross-purposes, Miss Allamont. Sir Osborne sent a groom here two days ago to allay his anxieties on the question of your health. His letter concerns another matter altogether. Will you read it?" He held out a sealed missive of at least two pages.

"Oh. I beg your pardon, I did not know about the groom. Of course I will read it."

She took the letter from him and broke the seal. As soon as she unfolded the sheets and began to read the elegantly flowing script, her legs turned to water. She sat abruptly in a nearby chair, scanning the pages as fast as her eyes could move, yet taking none of it in.

Sir Osborne wished to marry her! Of all the unexpected and unlikely events, that was one she had never entertained, not for a second. How many years had they known each other, and exchanged polite greetings and even danced together on many occasions, and yet he had never shown the slightest interest in her? It was of all things the most bizarre. Yet there it was, indisputably an offer of marriage. She read it once, then began again, and it still said the same — Sir Osborne Hardy of Brinford Manor in the county of Brinshire wished to marry her.

She looked across at Mr Merton, still politely standing. "I beg your pardon, my manners have flown away. Pray sit down, Mr Merton. You are aware of the contents of this letter, I take it?"

"I am."

"Naturally you are. I daresay you wrote it for him."

"I am his secretary," he said mildly.

She smiled wryly. "So you are. Tell me, Mr Merton, in your opinion how should I answer this?"

"Why, however you wish to answer, Miss Allamont. It is an offer of marriage. You may accept it or decline it, as pleases you." When she said nothing, he went on, "A title, a fine manor, a good income — it is a very good offer."

That made her laugh. "You do not need to enumerate the advantages of the match, Mr Merton. It is an exceptionally good offer, better than I have any right to expect at my advanced age. But is he in earnest?"

"It would be a foolish man indeed who offers for a lady and is *not* in earnest."

Mary rose and paced across the room, causing him to jump to his feet too. As she passed in front of the window, spring sunshine cast a warmth over her, the shaft of brilliant light dazzling her for a moment.

Spinning to face him, she said, "It is a generous impulse, but tell me honestly — does it arise purely from pity, after my abject appearance in the rain? He feels sorry for me, so he would rescue me from my miserable life, is that it?"

"I would say, rather, that your distress that day caused him to see you clearly for the first time. We are all at our best in the ballroom, wearing our finest clothes and widest smiles like a carapace to hide our true selves. But that day in the rain, Osborne saw you as a *person*, and one moreover who is hectored by a mother just as he is. He saw you as a kindred spirit, Miss Allamont. He genuinely wishes to marry you."

She was silent for a while. He waited patiently, the only sound in the room the ticking of the longcase clock in the corner, and the shifting coals on the fire.

"Mr Merton, if you look in that sideboard, you will find a bottle of brandy. I feel the need of a restorative. And please pour a glass for yourself."

"You have had a shock," he said, as he prepared their drinks. "You will need time to think about this, and to discuss it with your father."

"There is nothing for me to think about," Mary said, sipping her brandy, grateful for its bracing warmth in her throat. "I cannot refuse, Mr Merton. My life here is intolerable, and only marriage will allow me to escape it honourably. But tell me your honest opinion, do you believe that this marriage will make Sir Osborne happy?"

He gazed at her above the brandy glass in his hands. "Osborne is a gentle soul, Miss Allamont. He asks very little of the world. If, as his wife, you can provide him with a calm home, shelter him from his mother and sisters, and be a friend to him, he will be perfectly happy."

~~~~~

"There is still time to change your mind," her father said as the carriage rattled through the streets of Brinchester. "Sir Osborne is an odd sort of man, and no one would think the worse of you if—"

"I shall not change my mind," Mary said.

Her father sighed, and she turned away to avoid his reproachful face. He had been so happy when she had secured Lord Kilbraith last autumn, and so devastated when it had all turned to dust. Now, beyond all hope, she had another fine match and yet he was not pleased about it.

As if today would not be difficult enough. It would be her first meeting with Sir Osborne since she had accepted his offer, and her first visit to Brinford Manor as his betrothed. Her father had the relatively easy task of discussing settlements with Sir Osborne, whereas she had to assert her authority over Lady Hardy, who would not be willing to concede so much as an inch. It was too bad of Papa to be cross, just when she most needed his support.

"Some other means might be found to get you away from Vivienne, if you feel so strongly about it. We could—"

"No! What is the *matter* with you, Papa? He is a baronet with a fortune to his name — why can you not be pleased for me?"
~~~~~

"It is a marriage of convenience, nothing more," he shot back. "Sir Osborne cares nothing for you, nothing at all. His mother has hounded him to marry, and he is doing his duty, no more than that. Oh, Mary! I hate to think of you cooped up in that place with a man like Hardy, and all his female relatives, and Daniel Merton, too. It is an odd arrangement, very odd. Of course you will be rich and have a title, your life will be one of the greatest luxury, but you are throwing yourself away, marrying a man like that."

"I disagree," she said, her anger not entirely concealed, and he lapsed into a sulky silence which lasted the rest of the journey.

How could she help being angry? She had never wanted to marry, not Sir Osborne, not Lord Kilbraith, nor any of the several suitors over the years not deterred by her lack of fortune. Had she not been quite content to keep house for her father at Willowbye? Her step-mother had forced her into taking a step distasteful to her in the extreme.

How could she bear to be a wife, to be subject to a man in every way? Men were evil, and marriage a kind of slavery. She would be mistress of the house, her will law in domestic matters, and she would be provided with every comfort that money could buy, yet she must submit to the will of her husband.

She shook her head in bemusement at her cousins, who fell happily in love, entering matrimony with nothing but adoration for their husbands, and they seemed to be content with their lot. But for Mary, that could never happen, and marriage would be, at best, a disagreeable necessity.

Sir Osborne and Mr Merton were on the steps of the Manor waiting to greet them, Merton in his usual sober indoor attire, and Sir Osborne bundled up in hat and gloves, and a massive greatcoat with many capes. To one side, all the staff lined up with military precision, a formidable array. Of Lady Hardy and the Miss Hardys there was no sign.

As the carriage rolled to a halt, it was Daniel Merton who came forward to open the carriage door and assist Mary to alight. Behind him, Sir Osborne stood, swaying from one foot to the other, his hands twisting restlessly. He was not above average height, and very thin, the fraction of his face visible behind the concealing scarves as white as flour. His expression was anxious, but he was never less than polite, so he stepped forward gamely.

"Miss Allamont — delighted, quite delighted!" And then there was definite panic in his face.

Mary was rather amused to see such an urbane man, who spent part of every year in London for the season and had travelled widely, lost for words. He was not a great conversationalist, but he usually had the social niceties at his fingertips. But this was not a situation for which the *haut ton* or his expensive tutors had prepared him. How does one greet for the first time the woman to whom one is now engaged?

"Sir Osborne, how are you?" Mary said calmly.

The panic ebbed slightly. "Ah — tolerably well, Miss Allamont, apart from a little cough in the mornings. Nothing at all, I'm sure, but m'mother worries so, and she would have Torrington out to cup me. Quite insisted. Hate it, m'self, but must be done."

"You must always take the advice of your physician, Sir Osborne. He knows best, after all. Bleeding is most unpleasant, but so helpful in unusual cases, I understand."

"Oh. Unusual — indeed, I believe it *is* an unusual case. Ah, Mr Allamont. Delighted to see you. Not brought the charming Mrs Allamont with you?"

"We thought it better to leave the charming Mrs Allamont at home on this occasion."

"A pity. But let us not stand out in this wind any longer. Far too cold to dally."

It took some time for Sir Osborne to divest himself of his many outdoor garments. The removal of the greatcoat revealed breeches and stockings, a well-cut coat and one of his many splendid waistcoats, for Sir Osborne was nothing if not a credit to his tailor. Apart from the vividly-coloured waistcoat, his style was fashionably unostentatious, although perhaps better suited to the town than the country. But then he never rode, and was not prone to striding about the muddy lanes. Mary had never been particularly fashionable herself, so she had no fault to find with her betrothed's appearance.

The ladies of the household awaited them in state in the imposing Gold Salon, a depressingly over-decorated and over-furnished room with a glass dome, so large that the entire Dower House could probably fit into it. Mary had never seen the room before, but if the choice was intended to overawe her, she was determined that such a strategy would fail. She would, after all, soon be mistress of Brinford Manor. She walked in on Sir Osborne's arm with her head high, as if the house were already hers.

Lady Hardy stared unsmilingly at her, as she made her curtsy. "Miss Allamont."

"Lady Hardy. Miss Hardy. Miss Clarissa."

But these were not all the hostile faces looking her up and down. She turned enquiringly to Sir Osborne.

"Ah. These are m'sisters, you know. My *other* sisters. Lady Slocombe. Mrs Mansfield. This is Miss Mary Allamont. My future wife."

"We shall see about *that*," said Lady Hardy, and the four sisters nodded their heads in unison.

Mary sighed inwardly. This day was turning out to be even more difficult than she had feared.

4: Italy

Mary sat on a chair with a seat so padded that her feet barely touched the ground. It was a better choice than the one she had been offered by Lady Hardy, however, which was barely higher than a footstool. Instead of sitting low to the ground, with the five Hardy ladies looking down on her, now Mary had the advantage of them, for they, on their sofas, were lower than she was.

The gentlemen had escaped as soon as they could, leaving her with five implacable faces.

"Now, Miss Allamont, let us talk plainly," Lady Hardy said in stern tones. "This just will not do. Whatever means you have used to inveigle Osborne into a proposal, you must desist at once. He is to marry Miss Grantham."

"I am sorry to disoblige you, my lady, but I fully intend to marry Sir Osborne. I have not inveigled him, whatever manner of subterfuge that may be, and the choice is entirely his own. Therefore I see no reason not to accept his most obliging offer."

"My son is a baronet, may I remind you! He is a man of consequence, and it is hardly fitting for him to marry a jumped-up nobody like you. Who are the Allamonts, after all? Only two generations from trade, and even the recent generations not all they should be."

Mary took a deep breath. "Lady Hardy, few of us are so long-established in good society that we can be over-scrupulous about others."

This was a gamble, for Mary had little but hearsay to inform her concerning Lady Hardy's own background. That she had been a governess when she had attracted the notice of Sir Rupert Hardy was well known, but her life before that was a matter of much conjecture and speculation, and there were many rumours about the manner in which she had secured her husband.

Lady Hardy was red with anger. "You are insolent, young lady! You have no right to marry my son and—"

"Forgive me, but I must ask you to refrain from further comment on this subject, which cannot be fruitful. Shall we talk about accommodation?"

"Accommodation?" Lady Hardy said faintly.

Mary thought it quite likely that no one had ever spoken to Lady Hardy in such a manner before, but she was determined not to back down. She consciously kept her voice level, with no hint of anger. Or gloating — how easy it would be to gloat, but she must resist. "I understand there is no Dower House at the Manor, is that so?"

Lady Hardy was too outraged to formulate a reply, but the eldest of the sisters, Miss Hardy, said, "Oh indeed, no Dower House. There never has been one, you know. The west wing is known as the dower wing, and that is where the Dowager... where the Dowager... Oh, I beg your pardon, Philippa."

If looks could kill, then poor Miss Hardy would have been dead on the spot. Four faces turned towards her in ire, four pairs of eyes glared at her.

"Thank you, Miss Hardy," Mary said. "That sounds ideal. I have no objection at all to you continuing to live in the Manor for the time being, my lady, and naturally Miss Hardy and Miss Clarissa will always have a home here. However, we may need to consider the provision of a Dower House at some point in the future."

"You would throw me out of my own home?" Lady Hardy said, the anger shifting in an instant to fear. "But I—"

"It is usual when a man marries that his mother moves out," Mary said placidly, her calm tones in sharp contrast to Lady Hardy's shrill voice. "There can only be one mistress in a house, and a Dower House is the accepted solution. In this case, I am prepared to make an exception."

Lady Hardy's eyes narrowed, and she looked at Mary speculatively. "One might also say that there should only be one master, too."

"Indeed?" Mary said, although she guessed where this line of thought might be leading.

"My son should be master in his own house, but he is led by the nose by his so-called friend. If you wish to make changes, there is the place you should look, Miss Allamont. Whatever you may think of *us*, we are driven solely by Osborne's best interests, whereas Daniel Merton cares only for himself."

"He is a parasite," Lady Slocombe said with distaste, and the others nodded sagely.

"But such a pleasant young man," Miss Hardy murmured, almost inaudibly.

"That is a matter for Sir Osborne to decide," Mary said. "He may choose his own friends, I believe. And now, perhaps you would be so good as to show me the principal rooms." She knew exactly which rooms the Dowager would most wish to show her. "I should like to look at the nursery suite, as well."

"Oh, the nursery!" said Miss Hardy, pressing her hands together in excitement. "Oh, Philippa, *do* show Miss Allamont the nursery. It still has all Osborne's things, Miss Allamont. You will not need anything at all, for it is perfectly well equipped already. The nursery, sisters! That will be so delightful!"

Even Lady Hardy managed a small smile at the prospect.

~~~~~

There was one advantage in having a French step-mother, Mary discovered, and that was her instinctive sense of style. Now that the wedding was settled and an early date set, for there was no point in waiting when both parties were of age, Mary was swept up into a whirlwind of warehouses and seamstresses and milliners and the fashionable *modistes* who turned her step-mother out in such style and were now happy to do the same for her.
~~~~~

Suddenly, it seemed, her step-mother was her friend, anxious to oblige. Nothing was too much trouble for a daughter who had been the lowest creature on the earth just days before, but now was poised to marry a baronet. Where her proposed marriage to Lord Kilbraith, the heir to an earldom, had elicited nothing but amused disdain from Vivienne, now she was respectful and eager to please.

"You must have the very best, *ma cherie*, especially for your come-out in London. The very best! You will be presented at court, and invited everywhere. So exciting! You will obtain the best fabrics from the warehouses there, and I shall be happy to attend you to advise, for Lady Hardy has not the least idea of fashion, none whatsoever. You will remember? Your papa and I shall be very happy to come to you whenever you wish. And you will entertain a great deal at the Manor, I make no doubt."

"Only if Sir Osborne wishes it, Mama. He likes a quiet life."

"Pfft. That was well enough when he was a bachelor, but a married man must honour his wife by showing her off to the world."

It was pathetic, and Mary could not find it in her heart to be charitable towards her step-mother, not after being the recipient of so many insults. She was marrying to escape Vivienne, after all, and inviting her to London would entirely defeat the purpose. But she had no wish to destroy their transient harmony, so she kept silent and meekly allowed herself to be fitted for new gowns and bonnets and pelisses and riding habits, without comment. Anything not to her taste could be reworked later. But on one occasion, she could not help protesting.

"This is quite outlandish, Mama," Mary said, as she stood on a stool while the *modiste's* three assistants crawled on the floor pinning the hem of a stunningly wide-skirted gown. "Are you sure this is the latest fashion?"

Vivienne and the *modiste* exchanged despairing glances. "It is for court, *ma cherie*. Fashion has nothing to do with the case, sadly. One must wear this dreadful style to be presented. Do you think I would dress you in such a hideous manner for any less a cause? But you must be presented — the wife of a baronet, just think of it!"

"You were not so enthusiastic when I nearly became the wife of a future earl," Mary said, unable to resist the jibe.

"Oh, Kilbraith. Pfft. He told me they never leave Scotland. No house in town, no season, no balls. What could be duller? And nothing of style about him at all. No, he was of no interest to me. Apart from the detail that he was so amusingly in love with you, and made sheep's eyes at you all the time, and yet you viewed him with such distaste. So vastly entertaining, but still, I could not like such a man. But Sir Osborne does everything as he should, and he dresses so well. You must be at least as fine as your husband, do you not agree?"

~~~~~

The wedding clothes were made, the new carriage was delivered, the banns were read and the marriage took place, with the tiny church at Brafton West filled to capacity. After a wedding breakfast at Willowbye, the happy couple returned to Brinford Manor to begin their married life. Two days later, they set off again for a wedding tour of Italy, accompanied by Daniel Merton, Sir Osborne's two valets and the rather fearsome French lady's maid Vivienne had found for Mary.

Travel was a new experience for Mary. Apart from two brief visits to London as a child to see an elderly aunt of her mother's, she had never left the county. On those occasions, she had travelled on the mail coach with her father. Now she travelled in a convoy of three coaches, one for herself, Sir Osborne and Mr Merton, one for the servants and smaller items of luggage, and a third for the bulk of their boxes. At the coast, they added an interpreter guide and a physician to their entourage.

"Cannot be too careful with one's health when abroad," Sir Osborne said, shuddering, as they dined for the last time on English soil. "So many strange maladies, insects of the most violent kind, and snakes! Even scorpions! Quite terrifying. So much heat and dirt. You must take the greatest care, m'dear. I know you have been used to wandering about the countryside on your own, and in England, generally safe to do so, but you must not attempt it there."

"I shall be guided by you, Sir Osborne," Mary said, smiling at him.
~~~~~

"Quite right, quite right. And Danny knows how to go on, for we had a wonderful tour of Italy two years ago, eh, Danny?"

"Indeed we did, and we shall revisit many of the same places, Lady Hardy."

"My cousin has given me a guide book to Italy," Mary said. "The wonderful Roman ruins and the frescoes sound extraordinary. I am so looking forward to it. My sketchbook is in my luggage, in anticipation of rendering some likenesses of the principal sights."

"It is a fascinating place," Mr Merton said. "So many beautiful churches! And the statuary and great paintings are outstanding. For myself, I enjoy the journeys between the great cities, too, for the country is quite different there and there is much of interest to be observed. Sir Osborne likes to sleep in the coach, but I love to see the peasants at their work, and the tiny villages along the way."

"I cannot wait to be there!" Mary said. "You must point out everything of interest to me, Mr Merton, no matter how trifling. I want to see and remember it all."

"But the heat!" Sir Osborne said. "Beware of the heat, m'dear. Be sure to rest during the hottest hours."

"I shall certainly do so."

The journey was trying, as long journeys always were, but Sir Osborne spared no expense in procuring the best of everything. This meant that the discomfort was as small as was possible for travel which involved sea crossings and foreign countries. Mary had never in her life been treated so well, but then the daughter of an impoverished provincial gentleman was not to be compared with the wife of a wealthy baronet. She had only the vaguest idea of Sir Osborne's fortune, but her father had emerged from his discussions very well satisfied.

They started at Naples, gradually working their way north by way of Rome and then to Florence before the worst of the heat afflicted the country. Sir Osborne knew nothing of art and had no interest in learning, but he was happy to sit in a shady spot in one piazza or another, watching the colourful life of the city pass by, while Mary and Daniel Merton and the guide moved from church to ruin to palazzo like bees in a flowerbed.

One morning, when Sir Osborne was feeling a little unwell and had chosen to stay in his bed for the morning, Mary and Daniel ventured forth to revisit a church they had seen a few days earlier so that Mary might attempt a likeness of the frescoes. Daniel's Italian was more than adequate for such an enterprise, so the interpreter was left behind.

Mary loved Italian churches, a cool respite from the outside heat. Whereas English churches had a dank, unpleasant chill, even in the height of summer, here the air was refreshing, and the great height of the roof and the echoing slap of feet on stone flags turned even a modest church into a cathedral. Daniel found her a chair, and she sat with her sketchbook, trying to capture the essence of the glorious art before her, entirely absorbed in her work.

Daniel coughed. "You must be thirsty, my lady. Should you like to find some refreshment?"

She leaned back in her chair, stretching cramped muscles. "I have been sitting in one attitude for too long, I believe. I am quite stiff. What hour is it, Mr Merton?"

"The clock has just struck one."

"Gracious! I had no idea. By all means let us move on."

"We can easily return here later, if you wish to finish your sketch."

"I think not. My small talent is by no means adequate for the task. I cannot recreate the beauty of the artist's vision, so my little drawings serve only to fix the memory of the work in my mind, no more than that."

There was a small hotel on the other side of the piazza from the church, so they sat on a marble bench beneath a fig tree while servants rushed out with fruit and bread and wine, and a small table to set them on. They ate and drank a little, and because it was so pleasant, lingered on, savouring the warmth.

In two days, they would begin the long journey home again, and there would be Lady Hardy — the Dowager Lady Hardy, now — to deal with, and all the endless duties that befell the mistress of Brinford Manor. Mary was not afraid of those. Perhaps there would be other things to fear, but her mother-in-law and her public role were not amongst them. But one fear could, perhaps, be allayed quite easily.

"Mr Merton — or may I call you Daniel? You are such a good friend to Osborne, that I feel you are my friend also."

His thin face was lit by a sudden smile. "I hope you will always see me as such, Lady Hardy, for I am entirely at your service. Please do address me as Daniel."

"You are very kind. You must call me Mary, also."

"I am deeply honoured, my— um, Mary."

"Daniel, you have known Osborne for many years. This is the third time since we arrived in Italy that he has been afflicted with some kind of malaise. Is that usual for him? I know he suffers great anxiety over his health, but is there truly cause for alarm, do you think?"

Daniel paused, brow furrowed. "He has occasionally been laid low, it is true, as everyone is from time to time, but as a rule any debility is soon gone. To be entirely honest, much of it arises from his own fears or those of his mama, and he is not ill nearly so often as he believes. On the last occasion when we visited Italy, he was well for the entire time."

"Oh, so this is indeed unusual for him?"

"It is. My lady — Mary — would you forgive me if I ask a most impertinent question?"

"Please, if it concerns Osborne you may ask whatever you wish."

"Well then, is it possible that he has... over-exerted himself?"

She frowned, puzzled.

"I mean," he rushed on, red with embarrassment, "he is so recently married, it would be quite natural—"

"Oh, I see!" Now it was Mary's turn to blush. "No, that is not it. In fact, if I may speak plain, far from over-exerting himself, there have been no exertions at all. Dear me, what a subject for so public a place! It is to be hoped that no one else here speaks English."

"A thousand apologies for mentioning so delicate a question. I daresay he is... um, waiting until you are settled at the Manor. But perhaps you would wish me to discuss the matter with him?"

"Oh, by no means!" she said hastily. "I would not for the world... Oh, pray do not."

"Of course, of course. Whatever you wish. I think perhaps... Shall we make our way back to the hotel?"

She rose, still blushing. "By all means. And Daniel — you will not say anything to Osborne about this?"

"Not a word, I promise you."

"It is entirely a matter for him to decide, and I would not have him... troubled about it. It will happen when he is ready, and as far as I am concerned, he may take as long as he needs to reach that point."

5: Mistress Of Brinford Manor

Mary decided that she rather enjoyed receiving wedding calls. Her return to Brinford Manor was enlivened by a succession of relatives, friends and acquaintances, all keen to reassure themselves that she had survived her travel to foreign parts unscathed, and, more surreptitiously, to determine how well the odd pairing might be settling into married life.

She sat in splendour in one of her new gowns in the smaller of the two drawing rooms, chosen in part because the colours were more to her taste, and partly because it upset her mother-in-law so.

"One always receives in the State Room," the Dowager hissed in obvious distress. "This is merely the ante-room. It is where one keeps visitors waiting until one is ready to receive them."

"I like this room better," Mary said. "I may use the State Room when I have made some changes to it."

"Changes?" the Dowager said faintly. "There is no need at all for that! Such a wasteful expense! It was refurbished no more than fifteen years ago, and has been much admired."

"But all brides like to redecorate, Philippa," Miss Hardy said, with her benign smile. "And the furniture is a little heavy, I have always thought so, but did not quite like to mention it."

"Nothing extravagant, I assure you," Mary said, with what she hoped was a reassuring smile. "Perhaps some new wallpaper, and I may rearrange the furniture a little. I shall ask my cousin, Lady Carrbridge, for advice. She has an excellent eye for colour."

"Oh, the dear Marchioness!" exclaimed Miss Hardy. "I do hope you will invite her to stay, Mary dear. Oh, here is our first caller today. Look, it is Mr and Mrs Wills — how delightful!"

Sir Osborne sat beside her, smiling and nodding at their guests. Whenever he spoke of Mary, he called her *'my dear wife'*, and patted her hand gently. It was all very pleasant, with nothing to disturb Mary's days, or her nights either. She could scarcely believe her luck.

~~~~~

To himself, Daniel called them the five witches. For a long time, he had seen little difference between them. Osborne's mother and his four sisters were much of an age, and, collected together, their harassment of Osborne was uniform and unremitting. But gradually he had come to see subtle differences. Lady Hardy, the former governess, very conscious of her position. Miss Clarissa, who despised her. Lady Slocombe, wife of a baron, and proud to outrank everyone. Mrs Mansfield, resentful of Osborne because her twin had also been an Osborne, one of several of that name who had died in infancy. And then there was the eldest, Miss Ruth Hardy — she was rather sweet, and often supported Osborne against the rest, but ineffectual.

And all of them, all five, despised Daniel with a deep and abiding hatred.

Naturally, Mrs Mansfield and Lady Slocombe came to see the returning bride and offer their collected wisdom on the management of the house and servants. Being visitors, there was no sweeping them off to the dower wing with Osborne's mother. They installed themselves in the two finest guest bedrooms and had the servants running up and down the stairs all day long.

It amused Daniel to watch Mary as she smiled and let them lecture her on the rotation of linens and the proper training of housemaids, as if she had not been running her father's house for a decade or more before her step-mother had returned. She seemed docile enough, but Daniel knew she was no timid mouse. She rarely responded forcefully but occasionally, when the witches goaded her too far, the claws came out.
~~~~~

One evening at dinner, the talk amongst the ladies turned to redecoration. Having criticised every aspect of Mary's plans for the State Room and the music room, to which she made no response, they tried again.

"You should begin making plans for the nursery suite, Mary," Miss Clarissa said. "Naturally, you will want to have everything in place in plenty of time."

"The nursery is very well equipped already," the Dowager said. "Mary will not need much extra."

"It is never too soon to be thinking about a nanny," Lady Slocombe said. "My own nanny is a treasure, and I cannot spare her, even though the girls are quite grown up now, but she may be able to recommend someone."

Daniel saw that Osborne was uncomfortable with the discussion, but he could hardly intervene on such a subject. Indeed, when the five witches were in full flow, there was no stopping them. He hoped the ladies would soon withdraw, so that he could soothe Osborne and restore some semblance of equanimity. It was fortunate that they had no dinner guests that evening.

Mary had clearly noticed Osborne's discomfort too, for she said, "This is not a topic of interest to the gentlemen, I think. Mr Merton, is your horse fit again? I plan to ride over to visit some tenants at Nether Hafford tomorrow, if the weather stays kind. You are welcome to join me."

Lady Slocombe subsided, but Lady Hardy was not to be deterred. "It is a topic that *should* be of the greatest interest to Osborne, however, for what else is the purpose of marriage?"

Osborne began to look panicked.

Mary straightened her back. "Lady Hardy, if Sir Osborne wishes to discuss any particular subject of that nature with you, I am sure he will raise the issue himself. Or you may approach me, and I will determine if the matter is of sufficient importance to trouble him with. At the dinner table, perhaps we may restrict ourselves to unexceptional subjects like the weather."

The Dowager's mouth dropped open, and five astonished faces stared at Mary, but Osborne's expression relaxed a little.

Composedly, she turned back to Daniel. "What do you say, Mr Merton? Is Willow fit enough for a short outing?"

"I believe he is, my lady."

"You will be careful, m'dear?" Osborne said. "All this riding — not at all safe. You must not ride alone."

"I never do, Sir Osborne. I always take a groom when Mr Merton is unable to accompany me, according to your wishes. I know you worry so, and I am very grateful to you for permitting me to ride despite your fears, for I do enjoy it so."

"Know it, m'dear. Would never deny a lady anything that brings her so much pleasure. Puts colour in your cheeks, too," he said, blushing slightly. "Like to see you looking so well. But never ride alone. In fact, might be better to take a groom as well as Daniel, in case of accident. What if you should fall and break your neck?"

"In that unfortunate event, not even twenty grooms would be the slightest help," Daniel said.

Osborne stared at him for a moment, then chuckled. "Ah, you are so droll, Danny, so droll! What would I do without you to amuse me, eh? You take the greatest care of Lady Hardy when you go out riding, you hear me? The utmost care. Should not want the least harm to befall her." Another chuckle. "Twenty grooms! So droll!"

The three of them laughed at the joke, while the five Hardy ladies stared in bemusement.

~~~~~

The advantage to having all of Osborne's sisters staying was that they formed their own four for whist. Osborne and his mother were both cribbage players, and it was perhaps the only time when she was not hectoring him about some deficiency in his behaviour. She was an excellent player, and with a certain laxity regarding the rules, she almost always won,
~~~~~

which put her into a mellow frame of mind. Since Osborne felt it was his duty as a gentleman to lose to a lady, they rubbed along very well.

When there were no other guests, this left Mary and Daniel free to play chess. She had found him a very astute player who almost always had the better of her, although she had rarely been beaten at Willowbye. The slow back and forth of turns allowed both of them to observe Osborne. He was such an open person that he could easily be read, but tonight he was relaxed, quite in charity with his mama.

"He is enjoying the game," Mary said quietly to Daniel.

He looked up from the board, then across at Osborne's smiling countenance. "Her ladyship is in a high good humour now. Most unexpected after your masterful set-down at dinner. *'Unexceptional subjects like the weather'*, indeed!"

"The separation of ladies and gentlemen after a meal has many benefits," she said gravely. "I was able to take her aside and mollify her somewhat."

He smiled. "I should very much like to know how you managed *that*, Mary. It is a trick I have never yet acquired."

"I confided in her my concerns about his health, and my fears that any agitation could be injurious. I may have suggested the idea that she is the very person to ensure that he is kept calm at all times."

"You are surprisingly devious," he said, the smile widening. "But are you truly anxious about his health? He seems much recovered to me."

"I believe he is. Mr Torrington is pleased with him, and tells me that the little cough that lingers is of no consequence." She blushed a little. "He too thinks that Osborne may have over-exerted himself."

"And he has not as yet?"

She shook her head, too embarrassed to speak. He took the hint, and moved his knight. While she contemplated her next move, she said a little too casually, "Who precisely is Osborne's heir at this present?"

He had been looking at the board, but now his gaze shot up to meet hers. "Oh... I see. A cousin, I believe. He has children... a son, maybe two. The estate is entailed, so the inheritance is quite firm."

She nodded, and moved a pawn, almost at random. It was such a poor move that Daniel took it immediately. She laughed at her mistake. "I am not playing very well, am I?"

"You may yet recover. Your position is far from hopeless."

"Do you think so? I am not so sure."

They both knew she was not talking about chess.

~~~~~

It was the third time Clarissa had raised the issue. They were standing in the cheese cellar when she burst out, "Something must be *done*, Mary. This cannot go on. Almost ten shillings this time. You are not taking the matter seriously."

"I do indeed regard it as a serious matter, most serious, but I cannot quite see what is to be done about it. Even if I were to look in every servant's room and find the exact amount, I could not be sure it was stolen. One coin is very like another, and even servants may have their own money, saved from their salaries or given by their families."

Clarissa clucked in annoyance. "The servants! Pah! It is not the servants, and you know it. This money only ever disappears from the family's bedrooms, and only at night. The servants are in their own quarters by then. No, there is only one person who skulks around the family's part of the house in the middle of the night."

"If you are referring to Mr Merton, he rises early so that—"

"Mr Merton!" she spat in disgust. "You are as bad as Osborne for thinking of Merton as a shining beacon of righteous humanity. He is a parasite, Mary, and always has been. And now he is a thief, too."

"Clarissa, Mr Merton has been here for years. Why would he suddenly start stealing? It makes no sense."
~~~~~

"Why, he has been displaced, of course. Osborne has a wife now, so he no longer needs a secretary, or whatever Merton likes to call himself."

Mary could not listen to such venomous outpourings. "He still needs a *friend*!" she said icily. "He still needs people about him who put his needs above their own, for there are too many in this family who do not."

Clarissa glared at her, then spun around and stalked away, head held high.

But stealing was not a matter which could be concealed from her husband. Mary made her way to the far corner of the family wing, to Osborne's smoking room, where he and Daniel liked to spend their mornings.

Tapping on the door, she waited for the call of "Enter!" before turning the knob and opening the door. "May I disturb you for a few moments?"

"Of course, my dear," Osborne said. "Always happy to see m'little wife."

He smiled at her with such genuine affection that it was impossible not to smile back. He was such a sweet man that she felt a great fondness for him. She was very fortunate in her husband, in more ways than she had expected.

"I am so sorry to disrupt your business affairs," she began, seeing Daniel sitting at his desk with paper and ink, the sealing wax at the ready.

"Nothing important," Osborne said. "What is it, my dear? Some crisis in the kitchen? Oh, I do hope the fish arrived safely. Looking forward to a little turbot, you know."

"And you shall have it, this very evening. But that is not what I wished to speak to you about. Clarissa informs me that small sums of money have been disappearing from the bedrooms, hers and your mama's, in particular. I shall look into the matter, of course, but I thought you would wish to know."

"Oh, very bad, very bad," Osborne said. "Daresay it will turn out to be one of the footmen. Have to be let go, I suppose, and where will I find another to match? Footmen have to match, you know."

"It is unlikely to be any of the footmen," Mary said.

"I think Miss Clarissa believes that I am the culprit," Daniel said with a wry smile. "She has been making pointed remarks for some time now — about how I wander round the house at night, and wondering aloud whether I have any cash to spare. I had no idea what she meant, at the time, but this makes her intent clear."

"Nonsense!" Osborne said. "Silly woman, Clarissa. Always thought so. Ruth's the only one of the lot with any sense."

Mary said nothing, but she rather agreed. Miss Hardy might seem rather foolish sometimes, but she suspected the old lady was shrewder than she appeared to be.

~~~~~

The screams woke Mary abruptly. A high-pitched wail, going on and on, somewhere above her head. A momentary silence, then more screams, followed by rapid footsteps and muffled voices. Then sobbing, more footsteps and voices, more sobbing.

Sliding out of bed, she hastily lit the candle. Pulling on a robe, she opened the door to the landing outside her room. Osborne was peering out of his door, and then Daniel emerged from his own room at a brisk pace, his robe flapping around him.

"One of the maids in the attic rooms, by the sound of it. I shall investigate." He disappeared round the corner to find the service stairs.

Osborne peered uncertainly at Mary. "Are you all right, my dear? You must have been fast asleep, as I was." He blinked at her, then visibly shivered.

"Are you cold?" she said.

"A little. Fire's gone out."

"Mine still has some warmth in it, I believe. Will you come in? I can make you a tisane, if you wish. Or some chocolate."

"Should like some chocolate. Thank you, m'dear."
~~~~~

Meekly he followed her into her bedroom. She pulled a chair nearer the fire and settled him in it, while she built up a good blaze and then bustled about making him a drink of chocolate.

"Never been in here before," he said quietly.

She looked quickly at him, and there was just a hint of consciousness in his face. "You may come here whenever you wish, you know," she said evenly, as she poured the chocolate. "For whatever reason. Should you want to talk, or have some company, or... anything at all. I am your friend as well as your wife."

Taking the chocolate from her hand, he said, "You are very good to me, Mary." He sounded sad.

She tried to keep her tone light. "As you are to me."

"Not feeling that... you made a mistake?" he said, his expression anxious. "Not disappointed?"

"Nothing in the world could be further from my thoughts, Osborne. I have never been happier in my life."

He brightened, sipping his chocolate. "Excellent! Want you to be happy, you see." He paused, looking steadily at her. "Want you to have... whatever makes you happy. *Anything* you wish for, you need only ask."

She did not look away. "I wish for nothing more, nothing at all. I am perfectly content."

"As I am, too." He sipped again, still watching her. "So well suited, you and I. Just the right wife for me. Look after me so well. *Understand* me, better than those silly sisters of mine."

"They want to fit you to some pattern of their own imaginings," she said. "I just want you to be exactly as you are. Shall I tell you a secret?" He nodded eagerly, and she knelt beside his chair so that she could hold his free hand. "I was terrified of being married. I had the notion that I would feel trapped, like a bird in a cage, forced to be some strange new person, and not me at all. But it is not so. I am still myself, and you are still yourself — nothing has changed, except that I have someone else to share my life with, someone who is kind to me."

He squeezed her hand and then, with a shy smile, lifted it to his lips and kissed it.

A knock at the door announced the return of Daniel. “As we thought, it was nothing more threatening than Lily experiencing the night terrors. She has been having trouble sleeping and Mr Torrington prepared a sleeping draught for her, to unfortunate effect.”

“He gave Ruth something to help with sleep, as well,” Mary said. “I cannot see that such remedies serve any purpose, myself. Lily would sleep better if she would not moon about after the footmen so much. As for Ruth, she *will* doze all afternoon. It is no wonder she has trouble nodding off at night. Daniel, Osborne’s fire has died down. Might I trouble you to see if you can revive it?”

His quick glance flew from one to the other, but he said readily, “Of course. I will have it going in no time. We cannot have you getting cold, Osborne.”

“Thank you for the chocolate, m’dear,” Osborne said, rising to follow Daniel. Then he added, as he always did before bed, “Good night and may you sleep well. I shall see you again at breakfast.”

“Good night, Osborne.”

She sat in the chair, made warm by his body, and listened to the murmurs from Osborne’s room, Daniel’s low-pitched rumble and Osborne’s higher tones. Only when she heard Daniel’s quick steps taking him back to his own room did she climb into her bed and blow out the candle.

6: Summer

Osborne's face displayed the familiar panicked expression.

"You owe it to your position in society, Osborne," the Dowager intoned. "A person of your rank must mingle with others of your station, and exert his influence for good."

"We are all a little tired after the wedding tour," Mary said in her most soothing voice. "Perhaps it would be as well to miss London this year, since the season is all but over."

"Tired? Hmm." The Dowager nodded thoughtfully. "But there is still Brighton to be thought about. The sea, you know — *so* healthy."

Osborne winced.

"But requiring another long, arduous journey," Mary said. "Osborne, can you manage a little more turbot? I do not know how Mrs Callon has prepared it, but I declare it is as fine a fish as ever I ate."

He shook his head, and coughed softly, the dry cough that never quite seemed to leave him. Mary thought he was even paler than usual, but apart from a little lassitude he seemed otherwise well.

"But the house in Brighton is already secured — our usual street, although rather superior accommodation to any that we have enjoyed before," Clarissa said. "We *must* go, Osborne. Everyone who is anyone will be there, and if we have missed the season, we cannot afford to miss Brighton also, or else we might be entirely forgot by next year." She gave a little titter, raising her napkin to her mouth to hide it.

"It would indeed be a pity to waste the house if the rent has already been paid," Mary said to the Dowager. "Sir Osborne and I do not care to go, but there is no reason why the house should stand empty. Perhaps you would be so obliging as to represent Sir Osborne there, my lady? And Ruth and Clarissa, do you wish to go? Lady Slocombe and Mrs Mansfield might bear you company, perhaps. Who better to maintain the Hardy name in society than Sir Osborne's mother and sisters?"

"Oh, Mary!" Ruth said, clapping her hands in delight. "Such an excellent idea, and so generous. For myself, travel is too fatiguing to be considered, but Philippa, you should certainly go, and Clarissa too, and I am sure that Violet and Winifred would be delighted to take the sea air."

"We should need one or two gentlemen," the Dowager said. "We cannot travel alone." Her eyes flicked to Daniel and back. "*Respectable* gentlemen are essential to ensure all runs smoothly on a journey."

"If Lord Slocombe and Mr Mansfield could be released from their other obligations...?" Mary suggested. "I cannot think of anyone better fitted for such a task than Sir Osborne's brothers-in-law."

"That would be perfect," Ruth said. "Quite perfect. Oh, you *must* go, Philippa!"

The Dowager pretended to consider the matter, but Mary was unsurprised when at length she gave the smallest of smiles. "I believe we could take Osborne's place in the higher echelons of society which are to be found at Brighton without fear of besmirching his good name. But you must write to me every day, Mary, to keep me fully informed of every detail of my son's condition. Nothing is too unimportant to be reported. I shall not rest easy at night unless I may be assured that my poor Osborne is in health, and has taken no harm."

~~~~~

The summer drifted away in a pleasant haze. Daniel felt as if he had fallen into an enchanting dream, a life free from all cares, where every moment was a delight. Each day, he and Mary rose early and rode out. Only the wettest of weather deterred them, although Mary's maid grumbled at the number of times her riding habit returned liberally bespattered with mud.
~~~~~

Osborne was no rider, and preferred besides to rise in leisurely fashion, dressing with his usual care with the assistance and advice of his two valets. Then the three would breakfast together before separating, Mary to attend to domestic matters, and the two men to deal with letters or the accounts or whatever required attention in the smoking room. Then there might be callers visiting, or the carriage might be summoned for them to make calls of their own.

Evenings were the opportunity for an excellent dinner, better by far than when Osborne's mother had had the ordering of it. Daniel saw the delight Mary took in ordering a fine spread.

When he complimented her on the number and style of dishes one evening, she laughed and said, "An array like that would have been a monthly treat at Willowbye. So many years when I have had to watch every penny spent, and eat only the meat that could be had from our own farm, and sometimes we would have no fish for weeks on end. Now I can put fish on the table every night, served in half a dozen different ways." She leaned across the table to whisper confidentially, "I am beginning to know Osborne's favourites, too, for although he never asks for a particular dish and eats whatever is provided without complaint, I have set myself to notice anything he particularly relishes. I keep a small notebook for the purpose, and each morning record what he ate, what he refused and anything he took a second helping of from the night before."

"And do you report all of that to the Dowager Lady Hardy?" Daniel whispered back.

"Only some of it," she murmured. "I do not think she needs to know that I am endangering his health with so much potted crab."

Occasionally they entertained or were invited out, but Osborne was fearful of venturing too far in the evenings, especially once the long hours of summer daylight dwindled away, so most evenings were spent at home. They sometimes played whist with Ruth, but when Osborne and Ruth played cribbage, then Daniel had the pleasure of playing chess or backgammon with Mary.

Much of the pleasure was secret, naturally. He might congratulate her on a particularly astute move, or praise her swiftness of play, but in reality he was admiring the soft smoothness of her cheeks, the long, delicate fingers and the expressive eyes. She was everything he admired in a woman — beautiful, quiet-tempered, competent, elegantly dressed without ostentation and with the intelligence to engage him in spirited debate. Her education had been lacking, and she was not a great reader, but she had acute powers of observation and was quick-witted enough to spar with him on any topic. Yet at the end she would always laugh and say, "Ah, you have the better of me, Daniel! You are too clever for me, I declare." What man could be unmoved by such charming flattery? It was delightful, and although she could never be more to him than a friend, it was enough to content him.

But eventually this pleasant idyll came to an end, with the return of the Dowager and Clarissa. With them came Osborne's other sisters, Violet and Winifred, together with their husbands and an assortment of children and grandchildren, who had also, it seemed, been enjoying the benefits of the bracing Brighton air. The Manor was suddenly very full, and the expanse of empty rooms no longer echoed hollowly to the tap of footsteps, as the pleasant quietude was drowned out by the chatter of loud voices, the squeals of the younger children as they ran about or Scotch reels played repeatedly on the pianoforte. Daniel and Osborne retreated to the smoking room, leaving Mary to deal with the hordes in her usual calm manner.

The first evening was rather trying. Mary had ordered an unusually good dinner for the occasion, and the two cooks had produced an array of deliciously tempting dishes. Daniel was seated at the midpoint of the newly-lengthened dining table, amongst the youngest Slocombes and Mansfields. At one end of the table, Mary had Lord Slocombe to one side of her and Mr Mansfield to the other. At the other, Osborne's mother had seated herself beside him, and even above the buzz of conversation going on all around him, Daniel could hear the drone of the Dowager's voice to her son.

"...by no means adequate," she said. "It is not good enough, and so I shall tell her." Here she cast a speaking look towards Mary. "You must have fires in every room at this time of year. A chill could be fatal. Have you spoken to Torrington? You must send for him tomorrow without fail. I am disappointed, Osborne. I gave her the strictest instructions, which she should have followed to the letter, and..."

No one else took the slightest notice of her, but Osborne was distressed, Daniel could tell. He was eating very little, merely toying with the crab souffle on his plate, moving it about with a spoon, even though it was one of his favourite dishes.

"And as to this meal," the Dowager went on, "I have never in my life seen such an array of foodstuffs injurious to health. She could hardly have chosen worse! So many vegetables, and shellfish! You should never eat shellfish, not with your constitution, but Mary *will* go her own way. She never listens to me, never. If I have told her once—"

Osborne gave what could only be described as a growl, more animal than human. He threw his spoon onto the plate with a clatter. "Say no more!" he said, so loudly that the whole room fell into silence. Even the footmen stopped moving in astonishment.

"I beg your pardon?" the Dowager said icily. "Are you addressing *me* in that tone?"

"Mustn't speak about Mary that way," Osborne said into the stillness. "My wife, you know. My *wife*. Must have some respect. Looks after me very well. Takes care of me. Won't hear a word said against her, not a word." He glared at his mother. Then, picking up his spoon, he added, "Besides, I *like* shellfish." He filled his spoon, lifted it to his mouth and, staring defiantly at his mother, swallowed the souffle.

~~~~~

Mary knew that she would have to pay the price for Osborne's uncharacteristic outburst. That would be another crime to set at her door, that she had so far over-indulged her husband that he had taken to shouting at his own mother.

The Dowager waited three days. By that time, Violet, Winifred and their extensive families had dispersed to their own homes, and the house had reverted to its usual placidity, broken only periodically by unhappy outbursts from the Dowager, her complaints followed now by a sniff, and the words, "But I daresay I am not allowed to express an opinion in my own house any longer. I see how it is." Osborne never replied to these barbs, but he no longer looked quite so panicked when she started one of her diatribes.
~~~~~

The Dowager said nothing at all to Mary. But one morning at breakfast, the Dowager's maid brought her a note, couched in the most formal of terms — Philippa, Lady Hardy would be pleased to receive Lady Hardy to discuss certain matters of the utmost import. Mary was to attend the Dowager in her sitting room in the dower wing.

Meekly, Mary went, prepared for the usual assault. The dower wing, and the matching family wing on the other side of the house, lacked the scale and excessive ornamentation of the formal rooms, but the Dowager had done her best to introduce an air of grandeur into her new, reduced, domain. A heavily flowered wallpaper now covered the walls of her sitting room, and numerous large pieces of furniture had been crammed in, leaving little room to move about. It was as well that skirts were so narrow, for the vast hooped skirts of earlier generations would never have permitted access at all.

Mary sat on the sofa where she was directed, facing the Dowager on a chair so huge, ornately carved and gilded that it looked more like a throne. A queen in her kingdom, verily, even if her kingdom was much reduced in size. For a full half hour she lectured Mary about Osborne's state of health, his delicate constitution, every detail of his digestive problems from birth onwards, and how only she was able to appreciate the careful balance that kept the threat of immediate expiry at bay.

"I knew I should never have gone away and left him to the care of a stranger," she moaned, for at least the sixth time. "You have failed him, Mary, do you understand?"

It was almost beyond Mary's endurance. Each time, an angry reply rose to her lips, but she forced it down, for such insults were irrelevant, and instead murmured, "Certainly, my lady," or, "As you say, my lady."

"He is not well, not at all well," the Dowager went on. "He makes no complaint, for he had ever the sweetest temper, even as a boy — *such* a delightful child, everyone said so — but I can tell. As his mother, I know every nuance, every subtle change in him, and although *you* may notice nothing, I assure you the difference is very clear to me."

That was very much to the point. "Indeed, I *have* noticed," Mary said. "He is too pale, and afflicted with lassitude at times, as well as this troublesome cough."

"Oh. Yet Torrington has no concerns, it seems."

"If I may speak frankly, my lady, Mr Torrington is not much of a physician. He depends on bleeding and leeching, and if those do not answer, he listens to the heartbeat, then prescribes a tonic or a purgative or a sleeping draught, as he deems appropriate. For anything unusual, he has nothing to suggest other than weak beef broth and a glass of Madeira."

"There is nothing amiss with any of that," the Dowager said haughtily. "We have relied upon Torrington for years, and he is always very happy to come out at any hour, even for the servants, you know. Very sound, Torrington. Some of these newer physicians — one hears such tales, and one would certainly not wish to dine with them."

"Where Osborne's health is concerned, I do not think we should be so particular," Mary said. "I have asked Daniel to make discreet enquiries in Brinchester, and perhaps he may be able to find someone who can tell us more about this cough. If not, I think we should send to London."

The Dowager sat in silent dismay. Mary had never seen her at a loss for words before, but she waited composedly.

"Well," the Dowager said. And then, after a long pause, "Well. That is... concerning. And yet... so trifling, when one considers the matter. But perhaps—" She eyed Mary speculatively. "It may be that he is anxious about... other matters, for it seems to me that you are not doing your duty in *that* area, either. How many months have you been married? Osborne needs an heir."

That was plain speaking indeed, but Mary was not about to be drawn into a discussion on the subject.

"He already has an heir," Mary said quietly.

"Pfft. His cousin Rupert — a useless man, I have always said so. He would have not the least idea how to manage as a baronet. The very idea is unthinkable. It is for *you* to provide me with a grandson."

"Lady Hardy, let us be perfectly clear on this," Mary said. "The getting of heirs is a private matter, concerning only husband and wife and the One who holds us all in his hands. We must bow to God's will in this, as in every other area of our lives. If we are not to be blessed with children, we will accept that with humility, and I cannot — I absolutely *will not* — have Osborne harassed or made anxious about it in any way. He goes on much better when his path is smoothed for him, with no concerns to trouble him beyond which waistcoat to wear and whether it might rain or not. He is the sweetest, gentlest man, he is not terribly well and he should not be permitted to become upset. I am certain that you wish that just as much as I do."

The Dowager's eyes were wide, but she nodded once.

"As to the immediate question of heirs, the law makes adequate provision," Mary went on. "If you feel that the present heir is unfit, then he needs to be trained for the role. I understand that he has several children, and lives in reduced circumstances, so I imagine he would be glad of some attention."

"Attention?" the Dowager said faintly.

"Lady Hardy, who better to train a potential baronet than a person who has already done so successfully? Who but yourself is more suitable?"

"Me? You want me to make Rupert presentable?"

"And the children. They must be educated to their position, too."

And with those words, the Dowager's face melted from outrage into something more speculative. "Ah, an interesting challenge. Tutors, no doubt. A governess for the girls... But they live in Bristol! So far away!"

"There is plenty of room here," Mary said. "After all, the nursery is already fully equipped. I am sure they would be very happy to live in such splendid circumstances. Then you would be able to take the family fully under your wing."

"Ah!" The Dowager smiled.

7: A Nighttime Alarm

Dr Percival was a quietly-spoken man who yet exuded authority. He spent two hours examining Osborne from head to toe, assured him that he could find very little amiss, prescribed a diet of plain dishes, nothing too rich, and a gentle walk in the fresh air every day.

"Sunshine is what Sir Osborne needs," he said to Mary. "Sunshine and air untainted by smoke. That is the most efficacious tonic I can prescribe for him. Do not let him sit indoors by the fire all day. Rather, he should move about from room to room, and at night instruct his valet to leave the window open a little to allow any ill humours to dissipate outside."

"Is it your opinion that he will improve under this regime?" she said.

"I have every confidence that he will do so, my lady. There are no guarantees, naturally, for such a malaise as this must run its own course, and there may be temporary declines along the way. However, I am optimistic that your husband will in time be as hale as he ever was."

It seemed indeed that Osborne was improving. The encouraging prognosis lifted his spirits and gentle exercise each day gave him energy.

"Hated the bleeding," he told Mary one day at breakfast. "Always felt worse afterwards, but Torrington would insist. Never quite liked to refuse, because what is the point of engaging a physician and ignoring his advice? Always felt terrible afterwards. This fellow is much better. Very knowledgeable and up with all the latest ideas, you know. Thank you, Danny, I might take a little more of the kippers, if there is any flesh free of bones."

"You seem a lot more like your old self," Mary said. "I hated to see you so low. You never complained but I could tell you were not at all well."

"Never liked to worry you," he said. "Or m'mother. Terrible worrier, m'mother. She *fusses* so if she thinks I'm sickening. You never fuss, Mary. Perfect wife. Quite perfect."

He reached across the table and squeezed her hand gently, with an affectionate smile. Mary was too much overcome to say a word.

~~~~~

Over the summer while the Dowager Lady Hardy and Miss Clarissa had been away, the mysterious thefts of money had stopped. On their return, however, they immediately resumed.

"That is very clear," Daniel said to Mary. "The thief must be one of the servants who attended them. I have compiled a list."

A steady downpour of rain had caused them to abandon all thought of riding that morning, so they had retreated to the smoking room to await the appearance of Osborne at the breakfast hour.

Daniel took a guilty pleasure in these quiet times with Mary. When Osborne was about, her attention was all directed towards her husband, which was entirely as it should be, and for much of the day she was occupied by domestic affairs or her duties as a leader of local society, entertaining or visiting or out and about in the parish with the sick and needy. But these early mornings held no such distractions. Whether they rode out, or retreated to the smoking room, it meant an hour or two when she was exclusively his.

Very often they talked about Osborne, and how to manage his life to cause him the least upset, but sometimes, as now, they would mull over tricky domestic problems.

"I cannot believe it to be either of the ladies' maids," Mary said at once. "Bridgeman has been employed here for years, and Dorling was with old Mrs Hammerford for — oh, it must be twenty years before she came to the Manor. It has to be one of the grooms or footmen. Who else went to Brighton?"
~~~~~

"One of the housemaids. I would be tempted to agree with you, except that the Dowager has now gone to Bristol with precisely the same servants, and yet we had another theft two nights ago. It can only be Miss Clarissa's maid."

"Oh dear. It will be most unpleasant if we accuse her."

"Indeed so. Yet we cannot allow this to continue. There is one ploy we might attempt, however. All these thefts have occurred in the dower wing, or very close to it. Miss Clarissa and the Dowager are the most common targets, but there have also been losses from the Blue Room, the Chinese Room and the Peacock Room, when those rooms have been in use."

"All on the west side of the house."

"Just so, and all on the bedroom floor. So I thought I might keep watch for a night or two, to see if I can catch the culprit in the act."

"Be careful — do not take any risks. If caught, the culprit may lash out, and if it should be one of the footmen—"

He smiled and shook his head. "I am reasonably confident that it is Bridgeman, and I believe I can manage a small, middle-aged woman without undue risk to my person. Besides, I plan to ask one of Osborne's valets to accompany me."

"Two of you? You *do* fear an attack, then."

He smiled wryly. "Not in the least, but if I should be observed sneaking about in the middle of the night—"

"Oh, of course. Do you wish me to bear you company, also? My reputation carries some weight in this house, I believe. I am tolerably certain I can protect you from the threat of dismissal."

"Absolutely not, unless you wish to damage your own reputation as well as mine? The master's secretary and the mistress of the house wandering about together in the small hours?"

"Oh. Oh, I see." She blushed a little, enchanting him with her momentary confusion. "No, that would never do, I quite see. You are such a good friend to me, Daniel, that I forget sometimes that others may... misinterpret our closeness."

"I am honoured that you think of me that way," he said, but his heart ached at her words. Good friends... *close* friends, but how he wished he could be something more to her! It was impossible, for she was devoted to Osborne and could not be faulted in that respect — she was indeed the perfect wife — but in some tiny, distant corner of his mind, he yearned for her to be a little less devoted to her husband. And then shame consumed him. He must never listen to that deceiving voice of forbidden desire, never. Osborne and Mary deserved only his unshakable loyalty.

~~~~~

The tapping encroached first on her dreams. She was in the carriage with Daniel, with Osborne riding alongside, in the odd way of dreams, and the wheel began to make a strange banging noise. Then the sound became the discharge of guns, and there were highwaymen wearing masks racing alongside the carriage. Osborne fell from his horse with an odd sort of squeaking noise, and Daniel leaned across the carriage and said, "Wake up! Mary, wake up!"

She woke with a start, dazzled by a candle, to find Daniel bending over her bed, fingers to lips. "Hush, hush! Come quickly!"

"What is it? Not Osborne!"

"No, no, nothing to alarm you. I will wait for you outside."

She slipped her robe on and followed him out into the passage.

Again he put a finger to his lips. "Be very quiet. We do not wish to wake Osborne. Come."

She followed his flickering candle through dark passageways to the western side of the house. One of Osborne's valets loomed out of the shadows, where he had been waiting near Clarissa's room.

"Is she still in there?" Daniel whispered, and the man nodded. "Then we will wait."

"Bridgeman?" Mary said softly, but Daniel smiled and shook his head.

They had not many minutes to wait, before Clarissa's door opened and a figure in white emerged, a frail old lady dressed for bed in nightgown and cap, and barefoot. Miss Hardy, her hands full of coins. She took no notice of
~~~~~

the three figures observing her, making no sign that she was even aware of their presence, although her eyes were open and passed over the watchers as she turned.

"Ruth?" Mary's voice rose a notch in surprise.

"Shhh," Daniel said. "She is fast asleep."

"Then we must wake her," Mary said firmly. She could feel anger burning just below the surface. To think that all this time, the thievery was down to one of the family! How dreadful! She had cast suspicious eyes over half the servants, and had even been on the point of dismissing one of many years' excellent service without so much as a character, and here was Ruth walking about as cool as could be.

Yet she could scarcely blame Ruth, for how could such actions be set to her account when she was clearly in a deep sleep? But then it was odd that no such occurrences had been reported before, although she had lived at the Manor all her long life. And the thefts had stopped over the summer, and only resumed when the Dowager and Clarissa had returned from Brighton. It was very puzzling, and Mary had no idea what to make of it. She knew only that, whatever the cause, such thefts had to stop and therefore Ruth had to be made aware of her own actions.

Ruth murmured something under her breath, quite oblivious to the three figures watching her, and set off down the corridor in the direction of her own room.

At once, Mary ran after her, catching hold of her arm, and spinning Ruth round. "Ruth? You are walking about in your sleep. Wake up!"

Ruth gazed at her, her eyes wide open, her expression slightly bemused.

"Ruth!" Mary gave the older woman a slight shake, more in frustration than anger, but to her horror Ruth pulled violently away from her.

"No! No! No! No!" Ruth wailed, waving her hands about so that coins flew in all directions. And then she began to scream, over and over again, her voice piercing, so that Mary instinctively covered her ears. Through the noise, she heard Daniel's calm voice.

"Miss Hardy? It is only a dream, Miss Hardy. Wake up, now. Nothing is amiss. You are dreaming, nothing worse than that."

His soothing tones had no effect. Ruth screamed repeatedly.

Mary had just begun to wonder if she dared to slap her, or whether that would make everything worse, when Clarissa's door opened and that lady strode out in a vast robe covered in dragons, her head a fearsome hedgehog of curling papers, and some kind of cream covering her face.

"What is going on?" Her stentorian tones echoed around the corridor. She caught sight of Ruth and tutted in annoyance. "Really, Ruth!" Then she slapped her so hard that her head spun to the side.

The screams were abruptly cut off, as Ruth snapped to startled wakefulness. Silence fell, apart from Clarissa's heavy breathing.

"Oh," Ruth said, her hands falling to her side. A last coin or two fell from her fingers, falling with a metallic tinkle onto the other coins on the floor.

"Oh Ruth, you silly, *silly* girl," Clarissa said. "Whatever have you done?"

Within moments the house was in uproar, scared servants materialising from the back stairs, the Dowager peering timidly from her door, and Osborne, in a rather fetching nightcap, plaintively asking what was going on and were they being burgled? And all of them looking to Mary for orders.

"Mr Merton, please take Sir Osborne back to his room. Where is Dorling? Ah, there you are. Attend to your mistress, if you please. Mrs Timms, a hot posset for Miss Hardy. Oh yes, Bridgeman, smelling salts, an excellent idea. Clarissa, would you be so good as to see Ruth back to bed? Lily, help Worthing collect up these coins and put them back in Miss Clarissa's room. The rest of you — the alarm is over, you may go back to your beds now."

Gradually the corridor emptied as they went about their appointed tasks, and Mary lit another candle and followed Clarissa and Bridgeman to Ruth's room.

"I can deal with this now, Mary," Clarissa said. "You need not stay. Go and see to Osborne."

"Mr Merton is with him. He knows best how to settle him after any alarm."

"Even so, this is not your concern. Ruth is my sister. I must be permitted to care for her without interference."

"I shall not interfere," Mary said mildly. "Nevertheless, it seems that Ruth is responsible for the many thefts that have troubled the house these past few months. That is very much my concern. I would have an explanation."

Clarissa's maid, Bridgeman, was building up the fire, and Ruth's own maid was occupied with tucking Ruth back into bed, talking gently to her, as if to a child.

Ruth seemed bewildered and a little tearful. "I have not the least idea what is happening," she said plaintively. "Why was everyone outside Clarissa's room? Was there another theft? So worrying! What is to be done?"

It was a good question, but not one that Mary could answer without knowing why Ruth had taken to walking about the house while fast asleep.

"There is nothing to explain," Clarissa said wearily to Mary. "Ruth has been sleepwalking, and she can hardly be blamed for *that*. We will put a watch on her room, so that she can be intercepted in future."

"But why does she do it?" Mary said. "That is what I cannot understand."

"Such things are a mystery," Clarissa said repressively. "Mr Torrington will be able to enlighten us about possible causes, but it may be that we shall never know. Perhaps he will prescribe some remedy to provide for a more settled sleep."

"Oh, but he already has," Bridgeman said, turning round from the fire. "Doctor Torrington gave Miss Hardy some powders to get her off to sleep, like, 'cos she was having trouble settling of a night."

"Not the same that he gave Lily?" Mary said.

Bridgeman fetched the sachets from the cupboard where they were kept. "There, my lady. That's what Miss Hardy takes, but she's been taking something of the sort for years."

"Ruth?" Mary said, approaching the old lady where she lay propped up in bed. She was so tiny against the vast whiteness of the pillows that she looked like a china doll, dainty and fragile. "Ruth dear, has Mr Torrington changed the mixture of your sleeping draught?"

"Oh yes," she said happily. "He is very good, Torrington, and perfectly respectable. So important, do you not think? Such a *good* family. I had a little trouble in the spring when—" She broke off, looking archly at Mary.

"When I married Sir Osborne, you mean?" Mary said evenly.

"*Yes*, dear, that is exactly it, for Philippa was so *cross* all the time, and... well, she makes me so *agitated* and then I cannot sleep at all. So he gave me something stronger. But then in the summer..."

"Ah," Mary said. "The Dowager was away, so you were less agitated."

"Exactly so! I went back to the old type, which had always worked so well."

"And then she came back from Brighton, and upset you again," Mary said. "That is very clear. So all we need to do is find you another powder that is a little stronger, but not so strong as these." She did not, of course, mention the alternative, which was to send the Dowager Lady Hardy away from the Manor. It would be absolutely a last resort, but surely it could be avoided?

"Well, really," tutted Clarissa. "So all this is Philippa's fault, I suppose. Really! I should rather think we should look to the *true* cause of all the disruptions here this year."

"If you mean me," Mary said with a smile, "I am very sorry to disappoint you, but I am not going away. The Dowager wished Sir Osborne to marry, and now he has done so. We will all just have to learn to get along together, would you not agree?"

"Oh yes, dear," Ruth said, beaming at both of them, but Clarissa stared at them stony-faced.

8: The Grotto

The heir arrived, with his entire family in his wake. Osborne's cousin Rupert was an unobtrusive man, the sort who might pass almost unnoticed in any social gathering, to be forgotten the instant he was out of view. His wife was a timid little mouse, even more overawed by her surroundings than the children who clung to her skirts, their eyes wide at the huge rooms with their polished tables and the gleam of gold and crystal everywhere.

Osborne greeted his cousin with genuine pleasure, detailing the many excursions and entertainments he had planned for their amusement.

"So glad to see you, Rupert, Mrs Hardy," he said over and over. "And the little children, too. Cousins should better acquainted, always thought so. Delighted to welcome you to the Manor."

The visitors smiled and relaxed a little. The Dowager took them briskly under her wing, skillfully detaching the four children from their mother and handing them over to a fleet of nurserymaids, and whisking the adults away to be refurbished to her own standards in a luxurious suite. They were to stay for a month, initially, and then a decision would be made regarding their future.

"What do you think?" Daniel whispered, as they watched the cousins meekly following the Dowager out of the room. "Will they last the month, do you suppose? Will they run screaming back to Bristol, or will they be prostrate with gratitude?"

"Hard to say," she murmured. "Whatever happens, it will be good for them to see the estate, since they are to inherit it."

Daniel raised a quizzical eyebrow at the implications of that remark, but Mary was unrepentant. It was no more than the truth, and a situation unlikely to change unless Osborne himself changed his nature. It would be as well for everyone to accept that, once and for all.

Within three days, the newcomers had been dressed in the latest fashions, paid morning calls twice and dined out once, and settled into the Manor family as if they had never lived anywhere else. They remained quiet and deferential, and the Dowager accepted their repeated gratitude with a triumphant smile.

"So *appropriate* for the heir to be amongst his kin," she said with satisfaction. "I have always thought so, but my ideas are never attended to in this house. But see how well settled they are already, and the dear children so happy! Such a joy to have children about the place."

Mary smiled and nodded, ignoring the implied reproach, and forbore to remind the Dowager whose idea it had been to invite the cousins.

~~~~~

With the onset of autumn, Osborne's health took a turn for the worse again. His cough had never quite left him, but during the warmer months he had seemed to have a little more energy. Now he kept to his bedroom until noon, and Mary had the adjoining room turned into a small sitting and dining room so that the three of them could still breakfast together without the need for Osborne to dress and come downstairs. He was used to the familiar company only of Daniel and herself at that hour, for the Dowager and his sisters never emerged from their rooms so early. Mary suspected that even the mild-mannered addition of Rupert and Susan at the breakfast table was too much for him.

Constant rain made it impossible for Mary to enjoy her early morning ride with Daniel, and the lack of exercise began to make her fretful. Her only outings in the fresh air were to accompany Osborne on his circuits of the terrace, the gentle walks prescribed by Dr Percival. Keeping strictly to the shelter of the portico, and bundled up in greatcoat, gloves, hat and many scarves, Osborne walked up and down, up and down precisely five times, and all at a pace that even a snail would think slow, and which to Mary's mind was positively funereal. When Daniel was there, his light conversation
~~~~~

lifted her spirits, but often he had errands to run elsewhere, and then she had to curb her impatience at the slow pace as best she could.

One day, the rain had finally eased off and streaks of welcome sunshine peeped through the clouds. As Osborne prepared to go indoors, Mary said, "This dry weather is too rare to waste. Should you mind if I go for a longer walk about the garden, my dear?"

"Might rain again later," he said. "Clouds to the west are very black."

"Perhaps, but I believe it will stay fine for a while yet. I shall not go far, just to the grotto and then back past the lake — half an hour, perhaps. No more than an hour, anyway, and you will be reading the newspaper, so you will not need me."

"Of course, m'dear. Know how you've missed your riding this past week or so. Don't wander too far, will you?"

She agreed to it, and with a smile, skipped away down the steps and strode across the lawn, delighting in the chance to stretch her legs. Her steps carried her downhill to a copse, and then, ignoring the path to the grotto, on to the more extensive woodland that ringed the estate. There was a meandering path here that ran all the way around the perimeter of the Manor's extensive grounds, had she the leisure or inclination to walk so far. She had never done so, but she loved to walk under the trees, where the dead leaves and brambles and fallen branches stood in stark contrast to the well-ordered neatness of the pleasure grounds.

Here was a wildness, a oneness with nature, not to be found anywhere else amidst the tidy farms and orchards of this part of England. The only part of her betrothal to Lord Kilbraith to excite her had been the prospect of living amongst the rugged and mountainous beauty of Scotland. She could imagine riding Majestad there, galloping through the heather surrounded by rocky grandeur. She had been unspeakably disappointed to learn that Lord Kilbraith's county was filled with gently rolling hills and meandering streams, and was not wild at all.

She had turned back towards the house, rather guiltily, for she suspected she had been away longer than she intended, when a voice hailed her. She looked back to see Daniel making haste to catch her.

"Have you walked all the way to the village and back?" she said, seeing the mud caking his boots. "You could have taken the carriage. Your errand is for Osborne, after all."

"I do not like to send for the carriage just for myself," he said, slowing to match her pace. "It might be seen as taking advantage."

"Not by Osborne, nor by me, and no one else matters. I have heard the sly comments certain people make, but you must not regard them."

He said nothing, merely offering his arm. She slipped her hand through it and they walked on together companionably. She understood his reticence. It was easy for her to ignore the barbs of the Dowager and Osborne's sisters, but Daniel could not be so complaisant. He was powerless, a mere employee, and safe only so long as he had Osborne's favour.

"You need not fear for your position," Mary said. "Osborne would never allow himself to be persuaded to let you go. You have been his closest friend these twenty years or more, he tells me. He was suffering ill-treatment at the hands of the older boys during his brief time at school, and you intervened on his behalf, an act of great heroism, as he describes it."

Daniel laughed. "He exaggerates greatly, but it is true that all his favour towards me since stems from that short moment of rescue."

"And your continuing loyalty and good service," she said. "He quite depends on you." He said nothing, so she added, "And so do I, Daniel. I cannot imagine what I would have done without you these last few months."

He looked so embarrassed at the compliment that she said no more, but it was no less than the truth. She could not have coped so well with the abrupt change in her circumstances without Daniel's unfailing advice and support. How many times had she turned to him for aid, and he had never let her down? So dependable, and such a very good friend. Why, if he had not—

"I think it is starting to rain," he said, interrupting her reverie.

"Oh no! Osborne will be so worried! I have already been out too long."

"He will expect us to take shelter, as he would do. Why else do you suppose there are so many follies and pavilions scattered about the grounds? Come on, we can reach the grotto before the rain sets in if we run."

He took her hand and together they tore across the lawn towards the small mound which concealed the grotto. The interior was supposed to represent a cave, and the walls were indeed painted to look like rock. There any resemblance ended, for padded marble seats lined the walls, with marble pillars cut off at a convenient height for the placing of drinks. To one side stood a large wooden cabinet intended to hold glasses and decanters, as it would whenever a member of the family notified the servants of their intention to use the grotto. Today it stood forlornly empty.

"Not even a glass of brandy to be had," Daniel said ruefully, having searched with great thoroughness. "Ah well. Let us sit and wait out the storm."

The rain was indeed almost heavy enough to justify the epithet, and a sharp wind tossed about the trees in the copse, just visible through the curtain of water that separated them from the autumnal scene beyond. Inside, however, they were dry and snug.

"Did Osborne take his walk today?" Daniel said.

Mary told him every detail, and they talked back and forth about his state of health, and whether he might have walked a little faster today, and his appetite at breakfast.

When they had exhausted the subject, Mary said, "Any news from the village?"

Daniel hesitated, then, with a sideways glance at her, said, "There is much speculation about Mr Rupert Hardy's presence here." A pause. "People wonder greatly what it may signify."

"That is inevitable," Mary said. "Villagers are such gossips. They will get used to the idea."

"It does not bother you?"

"Not in the slightest." Was there a tremor in her voice? She hoped not.

Another hesitation, and this time he would not look her in the eye. "You are content with the situation, then?"

Her breath caught in her throat, but the sound that emerged was almost a roar. "Yes! Completely content. Utterly so. You cannot imagine… what a *relief* it is to find myself in such a situation."

"Oh, Mary! Your words grieve me beyond measure. Marriage… the married state… it is not so bad—"

"It is, it is!" she cried, hot tears running down her cheeks. "Men are *beasts* and I want nothing to do with them, nothing!"

Somehow, and she could not say how it happened, his arms were around her, holding her, rocking her, while she buried her face in the folds of his coats.

"Sshh, now," he murmured into her ear. "Hush. You have perhaps picked up a wrong idea about such matters, but if I had ever had the great good fortune to be your husband, I swear I could have taught you another opinion of men."

"No," she sobbed, "no one can convince me otherwise."

He went very still, and for a moment she thought he might be angry with her. But when he spoke again, his voice was soft. "Then something has happened to you, to injure you. Who was it? The man you were betrothed to?"

She shook her head. Perhaps she could have drawn back, even at this point, but the comfort in being held was beyond anything. So many years she had kept her secret, but here was a man — a *friend* — she could trust implicitly. So she lifted her face free of his coat and said, "It was Cousin William. I used to go to Allamont Hall regularly for a while, to visit my cousins and share their lessons and he… you know what he was like, how strict he was. Everything must be done to his way, with no deviation. My cousins all bowed to his will, but I… I would not. I defied him, time after time. So one day…" She fell into silence, and for a while her sobs were the only sound.

"You do not need to speak of it if you do not wish to," he said, and although there was a catch in his voice, his calmness reassured her so that her sobs lessened.

"Everyone was out," she said. "Some festival or other at the church, but I had not recited my lesson adequately, so I was made to stay behind. And when I failed again, and told him I would not learn it, he... he said I had to be punished. He tied me to his desk with chains..."

"Good God!"

"... and beat me, and then... and then..." His arms tightened round her, squeezing her, but it was wonderful to be held so. She lay against him as he held her, and opened her heart to him. "He did things... it hurt... He *hurt* me, Daniel, he hurt me and I could not prevent him. He told me I was wicked to make him do it. I went straight home, walked all the way across the fields because I could not bear to be in the house with him."

"Dear God! My poor, sweet Mary! It is as well that William Allamont is already dead, for otherwise I should have gone straight there and..." His voice was low, almost growling. "I would have killed him with my bare hands."

At these words, spoken with such fierce intensity, she lifted her face to him. "Would you? Truly?" The set expression on his face would have frightened her if she did not know him so well. "Oh, Daniel, I feel so much better for telling you about it. I have never been able to tell anyone before, but you are such a good friend to me, such a dear friend..."

He was so close, his face just inches from her own, and the relief from confiding her story made her giddy with a kind of madness. His gaze mesmerised her and she could not draw back. Nor did she want to. No one had held her this way since she was a child on her nurse's knee. No one had touched her as Daniel touched her now, his fingers gently stroking her cheek. No one had kissed her... she closed her eyes and let his lips meet hers.

Such warmth! Such passion and yet such tenderness. She melted into him, and it was like coming home after a long and arduous journey. It was a considerable time before, reluctantly, they parted.

His eyes gazed down at her, filled with joy. With *love*. How long had he loved her this way? And the delight in her heart was a match for his own ardour. Love... such an unexpected emotion, and so unwanted.

Yet she was perfectly calm. "What must we do?"

"It is for you to say." A hesitation. "Do you wish me to leave the Manor?"

"Not at all."

"Or we could *both* leave. Start afresh somewhere we are not known."

"No, no! It is unthinkable! It would distress Osborne too much, and... I wish to do no wrong, Daniel. Whatever is in our hearts must stay there. We have been good friends for a long time, and we shall continue so, except with an extra warmth that only we know of." He smiled at that. "But Osborne must be our first care. We can never leave him, for he needs us too much, and especially so while he is unwell. I wish I knew what ails him."

"Do you not have a suspicion of what it might be?" he said, so softly that she trembled with fear.

"Oh, do not say so! No! The physicians have not mentioned the possibility."

"They will not, until it becomes unavoidable. Besides, it is very slow, and he may yet recover. Many do, who suffer from... this kind of illness."

"Consumption," she said. "Let us at least speak its name. Even if it should be so, he may have many more years of life yet."

"I pray to God that he outlives us all," he said with sudden fervour. "I shall never desire his death, Mary, never, so I make you no promises. You have my devotion, and shall always have it, and your friendship is all I ask in return. And one kiss... each year on this date, if you still care for me, meet me here and let me hold you and taste your sweet lips again. That will be enough."

~~~~~
~~~~~

Side by side they walked back to the house and found Osborne. He was sitting by the fire in the smoking room, pale and downcast, his newspaper tossed aside. His face lit up when he saw them.

"There you both are! So worried about you, m'dear, out in all that rain. You did not get too wet? You must take a hot bath at once. And a posset... change your clothes, everything must be dry. Nothing is more fatal than damp clothes. Must take the greatest care of y'self."

"You are too good," she said, sitting on the sofa beside him and taking his hand, while Daniel sat the other side. "I am sorry to have alarmed you, but, as you see, I am perfectly dry. I met Daniel on his way back from the village, and we took shelter in the grotto."

"Ah, sensible! Thought you must have done something of the sort. Met Danny, eh... fortuitous. Takes good care of you. Danny will always take good care of you, m'dear. Such good friends to me, both of you. My best friends in all the world."

Her gaze met Daniel's and she saw there the same warm affection — the same *love* — for Osborne that she herself felt. She loved Daniel, but she loved Osborne too, that could not be denied. Such a dear, sweet man and she could never hurt him. Three friends, as close as friends could ever be, united in affection and never to be parted, except in death.

Mary rested her head on her husband's shoulder, her eyes on Daniel's face. Whatever the future held, for now she was entirely content.

THE END

Thanks for reading!

I hope you have enjoyed reading this book! If you'd like to know more about the Allamont family and their friends, watch out for the next book in the series, ***Grace: The Daughters of Allamont Hall Book 5***. You can read a sneak preview after the acknowledgements.

A note on historical accuracy: I have endeavoured to stay true to the spirit of Regency times, and have avoided taking too many liberties or imposing modern sensibilities on my characters. The book is not one of historical record, but I've tried to make it reasonably accurate. However, I'm not perfect! If you spot a historical error, I'd very much appreciate knowing about it so that I can correct it and learn from it. Thank you!

Find out more: If you'd like to know about my other Regency romance stories, contact me or sign up for my mailing list, my website is at http://marykingswood.co.uk/.

About the author

I write traditional Regency romances under the pen name Mary Kingswood, and epic fantasy as Pauline M Ross. I live in the beautiful Highlands of Scotland with my husband. I like chocolate, whisky, my Kindle, massed pipe bands, long leisurely lunches, chocolate, going places in my campervan, eating pizza in Italy, summer nights that never get dark, wood fires in winter, chocolate, the view from the study window looking out over the Moray Firth and the Black Isle to the mountains beyond. And chocolate. I dislike driving on motorways, cooking, shopping, hospitals.

Acknowledgements

Thanks go to:

My grandparents, Henry and Hannah Austin, who named their four children Amy, Constance, Ernest and Frank, and thereby inadvertently inspired these books

My good friends at AC (you know who you are!) who provided me with advice, support, encouragement and kicks up the backside, hand-holding and hugs, laughs and tears, woo chickens, tacos and tubesteak

My beta readers: Mary Burnett, Antonia Frost

Last, but definitely not least, my first reader: Amy Ross.

Sneak preview: Grace: Chapter 1: Diamonds

Grace sat with her head demurely lowered. Her feet were placed neatly together, her hands resting in her lap. She said nothing, allowing the impassioned young man to have his say. She had received enough proposals of marriage now to understand the proper form.

The drawing room was spacious, for Allamont Hall was a fine building in the generous style of the previous century, and he strode about it, hands gesturing to emphasise his points, like an actor on a stage. He told her of his delightful manor house in Wiltshire, and the hunting lodge — not his, precisely, but his uncle allowed him the use of it — and the rich farm lands whose rents paid for a most elegant and stylish manner of living, according to his description of it. He mentioned the two carriages he intended to have and the several more horses to add to his stable, and he hoped that, when she was his wife, she would have no fewer than twenty-three servants at her command, and wear diamonds and silk, and sit down to two full courses at dinner every day. He dined with twenty families regularly in his own neighbourhood, he said, and more in Bath, and counted some great names among his acquaintance — he mentioned one or two, in an overly casual manner. There was a living in his gift, if she should have any clergymen in the family. She should want for nothing, he assured her, nothing at all. Except for love, of course. Of *that* he made no mention, only respect, esteem, companionship.

When he had exhausted his eloquence, she lifted her head and made the little speech which repetition had rendered fluent. Most obliged — such a great honour — very sensible of the innumerable advantages of the match — the greatest regret — impossible to accept — so very sorry to be the cause of disappointment.

He grunted in surprise, eyebrows raised. Leaning one arm against the mantelpiece, he stared at her in bewilderment. He was a solid young man, dressed with more flamboyance than elegance, his cravat an impressively overwrought arrangement. "You do not wish to be mistress of Darrowhall, Miss Allamont?" His tone was full of astonishment, as if he could conceive of no greater happiness in life.

"I have no wish to be mistress of *any* establishment," Grace said. "I have not the least intention of marrying at present, as I have expressed to you many times before."

"Indeed you have professed something of the sort, but naturally you were not serious. All young ladies aspire to marriage, when the right offer is made."

Grace said nothing, hoping he would draw the obvious conclusion from her refusal— that this was *not* the right offer.

The young man had too elevated opinion of himself, however. "I must beg you to consider your answer most carefully. It would be foolish to expect a man, once rebuffed, to continue to press his suit, and who can say how many more offers you might receive? If I may speak with the utmost frankness, Miss Allamont, your age is against you, nor have you enjoyed the advantage of a season in London to prepare you for a role in the highest echelons of society, such as would make you attractive to the nobility. Viewed in this light, I do not believe I flatter myself in supposing that you will not receive a better offer than mine."

This presumption was too much for Grace. Straightening her back and lifting her chin, she said carefully, "You do indeed flatter yourself, sir. I shall never lack suitors, for it seems *impoverished* gentlemen are drawn to my dowry like bees to clover."

This was a little too close to the mark, for the young man's lips compressed. "There is no more to be said," he snapped. "I hope you do not live to regret this day, Miss Allamont. Pray give my regards to Lady Sara and Miss Hope. I bid you good day."

He swept out of the room. She waited, listening to the murmur of voices in the hall, as he reclaimed his hat, gloves and greatcoat from the footman. Then steps crossing the hall, the front door creaking open and footsteps crunching on the gravel, disappearing round the side of the house to the stables, for he was too impatient to wait for his horse to be brought round.

When all was quiet again, she picked up her skirts and skipped out of the drawing room and across the hall to the book room, banging open the door. Here she found her youngest sister, Hope, giggling over a journal with their cousin, Hugo. Hope was the prettiest of the sisters, and Hugo was a broodingly handsome man. As they bent over the pages, their dark heads almost touching, an observer might take them for brother and sister instead of distant cousins.

In a corner, Miss Bellows huddled with a book. Poor Miss Bellows! Once the governess to the six Allamont sisters, as they had left their lessons behind her role had dwindled over the years to companion and chaperon. Now, with only Grace and Hope yet unmarried, Miss Bellows had added the role of matchmaker to her repertoire. She looked up with hopeful eyes.

"Grace, dear! Well? What did you say to him? May we wish you happy?"

"I trust you will always wish me happy, Lavinia, but not, I hope, as the wife of such a grasping man as that. Who asked him to come all the way from Wiltshire to pay court to me anyway?"

"Oh!" Miss Bellows' face fell. "You turned him down, I collect. Poor man! I hope he will not be too disappointed."

"He will not repine for long," Grace said. "He has such a high opinion of himself that he will soon be pursuing some other heiress to grace his precious Darrowhall, and to pay for his diamonds and his twenty-three servants and two full courses every evening. He will not feel my loss for long, I assure you."

Miss Bellows sighed. "Yet such an *eligible* young man, and a very agreeable manner. A most pleasing countenance, too, and so obligingly civil to me, always, and devoted to you, Grace."

"Oh, stuff!" Grace said. "His devotion was entirely to my dowry. They are always so devoted to my dowry, these ardent young men. I know we are very fortunate to have such large portions, and it was generous of Papa, when he was quite miserly in other respects, but sometimes I wish he had not set up that mysterious account for us in Shropshire. At least then I would not be plagued with fortune-hunters like this Wiltshire fellow, with all his airs. You are too romantic altogether, Lavinia, if you see anything of affection in his manner towards me."

"Well, I never liked him," Hugo said. "He is not going to hang about and have another pop at you, is he?"

"Lord, I hope not!" Grace said. "I have no idea why he stayed so long. Not because of any encouragement on my part, you may be sure. If I told him once I had no wish to marry, I must have told him a hundred times, but he would never take the hint."

"They never do, these fellows," Hugo said. "Always think they will be the one to turn your head. How many have there been now? Must be a dozen at least."

"Seventeen," Hope said in anguished tones. "Grace has had *seventeen* offers, although the elder Mr Cranford proposed three times before he gave it up and went away quite broken-hearted, so perhaps two of those do not count. And I have had five, and none of them the least bit interested in anything but our money."

"Now, now, Hope, I believe there may be just a little exaggeration," Miss Bellows said. "Mr Dawson is certainly rich enough not to care about your dowry."

"Oh, *him*!" Hope cried. "I do not regard him as a serious suitor, for he is old enough to be my grandfather, or almost so. As if I could ever consider such a match. I daresay we shall never marry, sister. We shall be old maids together, and take comfort only in each other as we grow old, and be buried side by side in the churchyard."

"Well, that sounds very dull," Grace said. "I have not found anyone who suits me yet, but I suppose we shall both marry eventually. We must, for the alternative is far worse, and I do *not* want to be an old maid like Miss Endercott, and be laughed at by the village children. I wish I had been a boy, and then I might have gone into the army. Think how exciting that would be, galloping into battle with my sword! I should like it of all things. But no, I must sit with my tapestry or my paintbrush, or practise upon the pianoforte, and hope for an eligible man to rescue me from such tedium. It is so boring to be a lady! If only Mama would allow us to go to London. Just think how exciting that would be, and that is also where all the most eligible men are to be found. We could have our pick of them, I daresay, and surely one or two would be tolerable."

"But we are so *old*!" wailed Hope. "I am one and twenty already, and you are *three* and twenty! Who will want us when we have been out for years and years?"

"You refine too much upon it," Miss Bellows said firmly. "Although it is a pity Lady Sara will not permit you to stay with your sister now and then. The Marchioness would soon find husbands for you, I am certain of it. Look how splendid a match she managed for Miss Graham, when even her own mama despaired of finding anyone suitable for her."

The sisters were silent, not liking to contradict Miss Bellows, but not quite agreeing that becoming the third wife of a gouty Viscount with a string of children and grandchildren could be described as a splendid match.

"You could always marry me," Hugo said, grinning. "Either one of you would do the trick, for then the Hall would be mine, you know, and I should like that tremendously. I was exceedingly put out when Papa suggested I take a look at the accounts for you and sort things out, but it has been excellent fun."

"You just like galloping about the countryside talking to the tenants," Grace said. "And to be sure, that *does* sound like fun. But Hugo, you will not be offended if I say that I should not like to marry you."

"Nor I!" Hope said. "For that would make you just as bad as any of the others — marrying for the sake of the Hall is no different from marrying for a dowry. Oh, how I *wish* Papa had not left everything so awkwardly! Such a strange will, insisting that we all marry in turn by age, and then, if Ernest and Frank cannot be found, the Hall goes to James or Mark or Hugo, but only if they marry one of us, and if *that* fails, it will go to the church and we shall be cast out of our home, and what will become of us then?"

Grace rolled her eyes, for she had heard it all a thousand times before. She was fond of Hope, as she must always be of a sister, but the dear girl always imagined the worst.

"Now, now, Hope, it will not come to that," Miss Bellows said soothingly. "There is still plenty of time for Ernest and Frank to be found, for I daresay they are far away and news is slow to reach them. Even if they are not, you will both be married before then, I wager, so it will not affect you, and if not, you will always have a home with your mama. Lady Sara will have the Dower House, and a comfortable income of her own, so you need not fear to starve, or need to seek employment."

"No, indeed!" Grace said. "That would be dreadful, to be forced to become a governess or some such. Oh, Lavinia, I beg your pardon! I did not mean... it is only that we are not suited to such work, you know. Not like you, so kind and patient as you are."

Miss Bellows smiled thinly. "I am not offended, Grace, dear. I know better than most the disadvantages of my situation, which is why I urge you both to marry as soon as you can. Being a wife, and mistress of your own establishment, and enjoying your own dear children — it is a far more pleasant life, I do assure you."

A discreet knock at the door of the book room was followed by the portly figure of Young, the butler. "Mr Graham is here, Miss Allamont," he said to Grace. "Shall I show him into the drawing room? The fire can be lit in a moment."

"Oh, if it is only George Graham, we need not stand on ceremony. Show him in here."

Young threw a glance at Miss Bellows, but with the slightest lift of one shoulder, she acceded to the arrangement.

George Graham was the only son of Sir Matthew Graham, a close neighbour and family friend. He strode into the book room with an impish grin on his face.

"How very cosy, I declare! This is treating me very much as one of the family. Miss Bellows, I trust you are well? Hope. Hugo. Oh, I say, Grace, I like this new way you have with your hair. You look just like a boy!"

"This shorter style is all the fashion amongst the *ton*, or so Connie said. Hers is even shorter. Her maid cut it for me when she was here last."

"Very daring of you," George said, winking at her. "I'll wager your mama did not approve, eh? But never mind that, for as I rode over here, I passed that dreary friend of the Donboroughs and he had a face like a wet week in Bath. What did you do to him?"

"She refused him!" Hope said, in a melodramatic whisper.

"I should hope so!" George said. "Can't have Grace marrying such a dullard, can we? She can do better than that, I vow. Much, much better."

~~~~~

George rode home in a pleasant frame of mind. The Allamont sisters always cheered him up — well, not Hope so much, for she could be unspeakably miserable when the mood took her — but Grace was a lively girl, and always good fun.

There was another cause for good cheer, too — Miss Dilworthy would by now be ensconced in her travelling carriage, together with her snooty mama, her maid and a parrot in a cage, which accompanied her everywhere, well on their way back to whatever God-forsaken county they hailed from. Lancashire, he rather thought. Or was it Yorkshire? Well, good riddance to her. He wished the girl no harm, but he was not about to become leg-shackled to so spineless a creature. "Yes, Mama. No, Mama. Of course, Mama. At once, Mama." Never a thought in her head that hadn't been put there by the formidable Mrs Dilworthy. He could not imagine what his mother had been thinking of, to suppose for more than three seconds that he would be enticed to marry such a feeble specimen.
~~~~~

Unfortunately, now that Lizzie was safely wed and well-placed to launch her sisters into society when their time came, Lady Graham had turned her attentions to the matrimonial prospects of her son. George was determined that it would avail her nothing. No matter how many Miss Dilworthys she paraded in front of him, he had no intention of being caught. Not yet! He was barely five and twenty. Another five years, and then, perhaps he would consider it, for he knew his duty as the heir to a baronetcy, but not yet.

He turned in at the gates of Graham House, pondering whether it was worth the effort of taking a gun out that afternoon, or whether the day was too far gone, only to pull up with an exclamation of dismay. A carriage was drawing to a halt before the front door. His immediate fear was that the Dilworthys had returned, but a cursory glance confirmed that it was a different carriage. Besides, it was a man descending from it, and mounting the steps to the entrance.

Hastily, George rode round to the stables, slid from his horse, and tore into the house, striding through the twisting passages from the rear and into the capacious hall, to hear voices from the saloon. Both his parents, and a third — the mystery man. Without ceremony, he burst into the room. Three faces turned to him as one, his mother tutting in vexation, his father trying not to laugh, and the visitor smiling.

"George! How delightful!"

"Uncle Jasper! What are you doing here?"

His uncle smiled, but Lady Graham said, "Really, George! Must you come in here smelling of horse? And where are your manners? Greet your uncle properly."

"Ah, no need for formality, Julia. I am glad you are here, George, for this is a family matter, and you should know of it. Your great-grand-mama's will has finally been located—"

"Good Lord!" George said. "After all this time! Wherever was it?"

"Behind a loose brick in the stables, would you believe."

George gave a bark of laughter. "I would believe anything of great-granny. That is just like her, to hide it away somewhere it would likely never be found."

"Indeed. It was fortunate that my new hunter took exception to one of the grooms, and lashed out with a hoof in just the right place, else we might never have found it. But it confirms what you have said all along, Julia, that the necklace is to go to you."

Lady Graham inclined her head graciously. "She always said so, but of course without a will... But I imagine that Lilian will say she was not of sound mind when she wrote it?"

Her brother had the grace to look embarrassed. "Lilian did say something of the sort, I confess. She set her heart on that necklace long ago, and heaven knows she deserves it, given what she has had to put up with from the old lady. My wife has the patience of a saint. But the law is clear, and the necklace is yours."

"The famous diamonds — shall you wear them?" George said gleefully. "How splendid you will look!"

"Regrettably, no one will wear them," his uncle said. "The diamonds have disappeared. Lilian has scoured the house from attic to cellar, as you may imagine, but without the slightest success. The maid has insisted all along that they were lost, and the worst of it is, she says that the last time she recalls seeing them was here in this very house."

"Really?" Lady Graham said calmly. "I cannot say when I last saw her wear them."

"Do you mean," George said breathlessly, "that the Durmaston Diamonds may be somewhere in this house? Or behind a brick in *our* stables?"

"It is entirely possible," his uncle said.

"Famous! We must begin a search at once!" George said, with a wide grin. "A treasure hunt — what could possibly be more amusing?"

"Oh, George," his mother said, shaking her head sorrowfully. "So frivolous! Sometimes I despair of you. When will you ever grow up?"

His father raised an eyebrow languidly. "It will do no harm. Let the boy search if he wishes. He must be bored now that all his friends are occupied elsewhere."

"Occupied?" George said. "Tied down, I should rather say. Dragged off to the continent, like old Wilson, or worse, to Scotland, like Macintyre. Poor Lannington is to be fitted up for a cleric's coat, and never was a man less suited to the profession. And the rest of them married, or as good as. Leg-shackled, and at only twenty-five. Desperate indeed."

His father smiled fondly at his wife. "It is not so terrible a fate, being leg-shackled, as you will find out one of these days, George. But by all means look for the diamonds if you will. I daresay you will find nothing but a great deal of dust."

"There is no dust in this house, you may be sure of that," his wife said, bridling. "Nor is there any corner neglected by the servants where a diamond necklace may be hiding."

"Then George will be disappointed," her husband said. "But it must not be said that we failed to look for the necklace, knowing it to be missing."

"Exactly!" George said gleefully. "I shall start at once — in the attics, I think."

He raced off to begin, his mother's protestations fading into the distance behind him.

END OF SNEAK PREVIEW OF *Grace*

Printed in Great Britain
by Amazon

31843543R00049